BONY AND THE MOUSE

Arthur Upfield was born in England in 1888. When he was twenty-three he emigrated to Australia, and during the First World War he served with the Australian Army. After the war he roamed Australia, working as a boundary-rider, offside driver, cattle-drover, rabbit-trapper, and cattle station manager. He got to know the Aborigines and their customs, and this material later appeared in his *Bony* novels. The half-aboriginal sleuth, Detective Napoleon Bonaparte, is based on a character Upfield knew well. Many *Bony* novels have appeared since the first in 1951, and they have also formed the basis for a television series.

Arthur Upfield died in 1965.

ARTHUR UPFIELD

BONY AND THE MOUSE

Pan Books Sydney and London
in association with William Heinemann

First published 1959 by William Heinemann Limited
This edition published 1984 by Pan Books (Australia) Pty Limited
68 Moncur Street, Woollahra, New South Wales
in association with William Heinemann Limited

© Arthur W. Upfield 1959
ISBN 0 330 27055 9

Printed and bound in Australia by the Dominion Press-Hedges and Bell, Melbourne

CHAPTER I

The Land of Melody Sam

Should you alight from the QANTAS airliner at the Golden Mile in Western Australia, travel northward to Laverton, then along a faint bush track for one hundred and fifty miles, you would come to the Land of Melody Sam.

Inspector Napoleon Bonaparte, equipped with a sound alias, did not travel by this route, as he had reason to enter Sam Loader's kingdom by the back door. It was a clear, hot and windy day when first he sighted the Land of Melody Sam from the verge of a breakaway, and there he dismounted from a horse and rolled a cigarette whilst contemplating the scene. The breakaway was the granite lip of a vast and shallow saucer, on which grew a mulga forest the like of which is exceedingly rare in modern Australia, where steel axes have been frantically wielded for more than a century. The limits of the forest in the saucer could be seen; the entire area difficult to guess. Outside the saucer, on higher ground, there grew only the sparse jam tree, the waitabit bush, and the spinifex, patched by large areas of surface rock, and larger areas of salmon-pink sand.

Over beyond the many square miles of this mulga forest, Bulow's Range lay sprawled above the eastern horizon, a pale-grey daub under the light-blue shimmering sky. Bony could see the burnt matchstick of the poppet head of Sam's Find, and the outline of the town of Daybreak surmounting the Whaleback Range, distant at least ten miles. There was the Land of Melody Sam, the destination of this traveller whose business was luring murderers from their holes.

The hot north wind ruffled the mane of the brown mare, and that of the packhorse burdened with saddle bags, spare saddle, and the gear of a horsebreaker. Scorched clouds moved across the sky, and not one passed over the face of the conquering sun.

From this breakaway were no limits to confine the soaring spirit of a man.

Down in the mulga forest it was different.

Again astride his horse, the man who was 'Bony' to all his friends rode through the forest which had aroused his interest in the story of its being. Before Cook first sighted Australia, an aborigine had stood on the breakaway and had seen, not this forest, but a vast flat expanse of spinifex dotted with jam-woods, gimlet trees, and ancient drought-stricken mulga trees of the broad leaf variety. Game was scarce, and he and his family were hungry, so he called the lubra whose job it was to carry the firestick from camp to camp, and with this he put the fire into the spinifex, for the purpose of driving into the open snakes, lizards, iguanas and banded anteaters.

Doubtless the present day was like that day, and the wind took charge and carried the fire across the saucer from side to side, burning everything to a grey ash. For many years the native trees had dropped their seed encased within iron-hard pods which nothing but fire-heat could burst open. They exploded like small-arms after the major fire had passed by, scattering the seed wide to fall into the cooling ash.

Quite soon thereafter came a deluge of rain and the seeds split open and sent their roots down into the steamy earth. A riot of spinifex and scrub covered the fire-bared land, and the mulga seedlings, proving the strongest of all, eventually gained the victory. More rain fell and, like Jack's beanstalk, the saplings branched and the weaker of these were eliminated, the strongest ultimately surviving to claim their own living space, and leaving no surface moisture for anything else to mature.

Of uniform height, about twenty-five feet, they were uniformly shaped, the branch-spread dome-like, the trunks straight and metal-hard, and matching the dark green foliage massed to give shade, unusual in the interior of this continent.

Bony and his horses passed over the parquet floor of salmon-pink and shadow-black. The wind hissed and raved among the topmost branches, and failed to sink low enough to reach him. The summit of the arches swayed; the walls of the arches did not move.

Nothing else moved either. There being no ground feed, there were no animals to be seen; and no reptilian life, and thus no birds. The entire absence of lesser trees, low scrub and spinifex, and grass, quickly made of it an empty forest. It was almost a relief to enter the clearing, and Bony dismounted at the edge of it and rolled a cigarette, whilst the horses nickered and raised their upper lips to the scent of water.

Bony found the water in a deep hole among a rockpile, and beside it a bucket fashioned from a petrol tin. Thus able to give the animals a drink, he loosened saddlegirths and boiled water in his quart pot and brewed tea. Seated in the shadow of the rock pile, he lunched leisurely and ruminated on his mission.

The case-files, the statements, the plaster casts of shoeprints, and the reports of detective officers, seemingly piled as high as this isolated rock mass, had given him a fairly clear picture of a community, and the shadow of murder which had fallen upon it. Daybreak, a town which had been created by one man, and seemingly controlled by this man, of unknown age and known to every prospector and miner in Western Australia as 'Melody Sam'. Three hundred miles from Kalgoorlie, a hundred and fifty miles inward from the end of the terminus of a branch line at Laverton, all this country unfenced, unused, never properly prospected, save a ribbon either side of the unmade road based on the railhead. And they called it 'The Land of Melody Sam'.

Daybreak, a one-pub town owned by Melody Sam. He owned the general store, he financed the mail-and-goods run from Laverton. He built and owned the church and paid the parson's stipend. He built the court-house, the school of arts, and would have built the police station, the post office and the school, had the authorities agreed. He did not, therefore, pay the salaries of the officials.

Melody Sam. A tycoon! A dictator! A political boss! There was only the one verdict provided by the records. Melody Sam was universally honoured, if not universally loved. It seemed that he had one failing in the estimation of his people: he would, without notice, march up and down Main Street playing a violin very well, but not the tunes in greatest favour.

7

And, too, he was a trifle unpredictable. No one could forecast the hour when he would start on a bender which might last many days.

Murders at Daybreak! There were three, the first that of a young aborigine called Mary, who was a protégé of the minister and his wife. In July of the previous year she was found on the footpath outside the Manse, having been killed with a blunt instrument. A month later a Mrs Mavis Lorelli, the wife of a cattleman living five miles on the road to Laverton, was found by her husband, having been strangled during his absence. In January of this year the third murder had been committed, this time the victim being a youth employed in the town as a garage apprentice. His throat was cut.

Now it was April, ten months after the aborigine's death, and nothing achieved by the police, other than a collection of plaster casts of sandshoes worn by a man having a slight limp in his right leg.

It was surprising how many men living at Daybreak had an injury to their right leg, and yet not so in a comparable community of bush people. It was strange that the local aboriginal tribe was absent when the girl was killed outside the Manse, for the aborigines were on walkabout and she should have been with them. It was also odd that when the remaining two crimes of homicide were committed the tribe was away on walkabout, and the policeman had to call for the services of a native tracker at Kalgoorlie, and he seemed to be useless.

It was reasonable to assume that one man killed these three people. His tracks were found on the scene of the second and third murders, and the plaster casts made of them identified him on each occasion. There was nothing more of any value. Motive was not indicated. No one crime was related to the others.

Suspects? Only one, a young man named Tony Carr, a teen-age delinquent of bad record, and now employed by the local butcher.

Quite an unusual set-up, and not to be resisted by DI Bon-aparte when in Perth on an assignment. On the evening before leaving Perth he had dined with the Commissioner and his wife, and the Commissioner had wished him luck, and the Commissioner's wife had urged him to make himself known to her niece, Sister Jenks, from whom he could obtain much local colour.

Sister Jenks! She had often appeared in the case records. Constable George Harmon, it would seem, was efficient and inclined to be ruthless. There was a man called the Council Staff, and Katherine Loader, Melody's granddaughter. A man named Fred Joyce did the butchering for Daybreak, and was stated to be guardian-employer and general tamer of the delinquent Tony Carr. And, of course, others, including a gentleman called Iriti, and his medicine-man, having the euphonious name of Nittajuri.

Too small a town, a too closely related community for a detective-inspector to enter in full uniform of braided cap and sword and spurs. Success would surely attend on an itinerant horse-breaker called Nat.

Bony tightened girth straps, and left the rock-pile, to be immediately intrigued by an arrangement of stones, obviously the work of aborigines. The stones were roughly circular and flat, each about the size of a white man's soup plate. Between each was a space of about two feet. They formed two circles joined by a narrow passage, that farther from the rock-pile being much larger than the nearer one. Twenty men could have stood without contacting one another in the larger circle, ten could have done this in the smaller one, and two men could walk abreast along the connecting passage, a hundred yards long. At the far curve of the large circle, three stones were missing, so that it was possible for a man to walk into the circle, and from it along the passage to the small circle, without stepping over the outline of the design.

An aboriginal ceremonial ground. The carefully selected stones had been brought from outside the forest. All were of white quartz. The upthrust of rock, amid which was water, was, however, of conglomerate ore, and thus evoked the question: why bring stones from outside the forest when a plentiful supply was to be obtained on the site?

There were additional points. The white stones were maintained in regular spacing, and free from drift sand. The absence of human tracks proved that the design had not been used for a ceremony for some time. It was a secret place which no white man would have reason to visit in a search for lost cattle, or on a kangaroo hunt. It was a lonely place, a magic place, and Bony was sure that amid the rock pile was the local tribe's treasure-house where were kept the pointing-bones and the father and mother churinga stones.

The spirits of his maternal ancestors came from the trees to whisper their taboos. Under the wind there was a silence, a watchfulness by the unseen, and sudden withdrawal from this place, of the world of living men. Bonaparte's white progenitors mocked him in these moments, called up his education, his reputation, to wave like flags before his eyes.

He compromised by leading his horses round the edge of the clearing to avoid crossing over the ceremonial ground, and so continued his journey through the forest, which never varied in aspect from what it had been before coming to the rock pile. The floor of salmon-pink sand, unmarred by the feet of man or beast, continued flat and unruffled by the defeated wind. Can a man disown his father and his mother? In the mind of this man, so constantly battled for by his unknown parents, the thought was created that in every one of these identical trees was imprisoned for eternity the spirit of a once living aborigine.

Bony must have ridden nine or ten miles since leaving the breakaway, when he sighted the eastern extremity of the forest, vistas of space appearing in the arches, and extending as he approached. Before him was no rock-faced breakaway. He could see the land rising gently beyond the mulgas, could see in the open spaces the snow-white trunks of several ghost gums.

The mulgas thinned at the forest limit, and the ground here was scarred by shallow water gutters. He found he hadn't done badly when crossing the maze, for he was out of course for Daybreak by very little when he saw the town on the curved back of Bulow's Range. A four-wire fence skirted the forest, obviously marking the boundary of the town common, and he rode to the right, hoping to come to a gate, and thus disturbed a party of crows settled on an object slightly inside the forest.

Well, it was early yet, and curiosity took him to the crows' find – the body of a doe kangaroo. And at once his attention was removed from it to the story written on this page of the Book of the Bush.

A barefooted woman accompanied by a dog had run into the forest. The dog had killed the kangaroo. The woman had fallen, and had lain on the ground for some time. Then she had crawled over the sandy soil out of the forest to the skirting wire fence. She was a white woman.

Bony urged his horses along the track of the crawling woman, coming to the fence, and seeing that she had crawled beneath the bottom wire, and so on into the open country, and towards the seven or eight widely spaced and ancient ghost gums. Tethered to one of the gums was a saddled horse. Bony cautiously followed the trail of the crawling woman until he came to the edge of the slight depression where grew the ghost gums.

Under one of them a woman was lying, and a man was bending over her with a long-bladed knife lying horizontally on his two hands, as though he were contemplating just where to plunge it.

CHAPTER 2

Distorted Pictures

The man was oblivious of Bony's proximity. The woman lay with her eyes closed, and her light-gold hair was draggled, her face stained and white. She said:

'Go on, Tony Carr, cut it out. You got to cut it out.'

'I tell you I can't. I couldn't do it,' reacted the man.

The long knife was lifted from his hands, and he was aware that someone knelt beside him before moving his gaze from the woman's foot, to encounter the blue eyes of the stranger. Swift in defence, he explained:

11

'She got a rotten splinter in her foot, and she wants me to cut it out. Look at it! It's dug in inches. She's been here since yesterday morning. She's had it. I found her with her mouth stopped up tight with her tongue 'cos of thirst.'

The stake was driven in just behind the toes, deep in the sole and almost to the heel. It was fifteen or sixteen inches long, iron-hard, a windbreak from a mulga.

'I want a drink, Tony Carr,' moaned the girl, for she was not yet twenty, and now her eyes were open, and golden, like her hair.

'Didn't ought to have any more for a bit,' said the young man, looking appealingly at the stranger. 'You mustn't give 'em a lot when they're like that.'

'You make a fire and I'll fetch water and things we'll want.'

Retaining the knife, an old butcher's killing knife honed to razor-sharpness, Bony brought a water drum, billycan and quart pot, tea and sugar, and a simple first-aid kit.

'I came this way to push cattle up to the yards,' Carr explained, as Bony made his preparations. 'I see her dog on a rock. The dog is famished, and then I see Joy Elder lying here. She says she was looking for garnets. Her and the dog put up a kanga with a fair-sized joey, and the dog chased the kanga over the fence into the mulga, and she went in after and landed her foot on a stick lying buried with the point just sticking up like.

'She knows that no one ever goes in there, so she crawled out under the fence and got this far. Couldn't pull the stick out, and couldn't walk with it in. A mug could see she couldn't. That was early yesterd'y morning. When I got here she can't talk. Tongue swollen that big. So I dripped water from me bag on her tongue till it sort of loosened up, like the blacks say you gotta do. You can't let 'em have a lot of water straight off. Look, mister, I'm slaughterman at the butcher's, but I can't take that stick out. What are we gonna do?'

He was solid, this Tony Carr; thick and wide and not so tall. His bare forearms were sunburned to match the backs of the powerful wrists and hands. His features were rugged, his eyes brown like his hair, and at this moment his face did not support the dossier Bony had studied when in Perth.

'We have everything ready,' Bony said. 'When I tell you to grip the ankle firmly, you must do that.'

Going to the girl, he placed a wet rag over her eyes, saying gently:

'It will hurt, but you must bear it. Think you can?'

'Yes. Oh, yes. Please get it out.'

Tony Carr didn't want this bush operation. Gripping the ankle as instructed, he felt her body rebel against the knife, heard her sharp cry, and himself felt the pain, and then felt the patient's relief when her taut nerves relaxed, and she gave a long sigh. On being asked to release the ankle, he saw that the gentle stranger was packing the wound with gauze.

'My guess is that the town is something like four to five miles away. There's a nursing sister there?'

'Yes, Sister Jenks. But Joy here lives at Dryblowers Flat. We goin' to carry her?'

'Better not try that,' decided Bony, glancing swiftly at the semi-masked face of the girl. 'You ride hard for the town and tell them to bring a truck and a stretcher. Tell Sister Jenks just what has happened. Now get going.'

The boy left at a gallop over the rough ground. The dog came and nuzzled the water bag, and Bony punched a dent into the crown of his hat and filled it for the famished animal. Testing the tea poured into the tin cup, and finding it cool enough, he added a little sugar, and knelt beside the girl and removed the now dry rag. Her large golden eyes were swimming in tears of exhaustion.

'This is going to be good,' Bony told her, slipping an arm under her shoulders. ' "Joy", the young man said. "Joy Elder" and you live at Dryblowers Flat. Now don't gulp so. There's plenty more, but we must take it slowly.'

When refilling the cup he heard her sobbing.

'I can't help crying. I can't . . .'

'Of course you must cry,' he told her. 'Here's a clean handkerchief. Cry all you want. Do you good. Now a little more tea, and then rest for a while. Your dog was famished too. Must have stayed with you all along.'

The girl nodded, and managed to call, and the dog came and crouched beside her. 'He bailed up a kanga in the mulga, and when I got to him, the mother was fighting him off and she had a baby in her pouch. It was when I ran to haul him off the kanga that I got the stick in my foot, and I couldn't do a thing about the kanga after that. So I crawled out to here, hoping Tony or Mr Joyce might come this way looking for cattle.'

'And you go out looking for garnets without wearing shoes?'

'Us girls don't wear shoes exceptin' when we go to church in Daybreak,' Joy explained, tiredly, and Bony thought that to talk was better than not. 'Janet and I live with father who's a dryblower. Father's pretty old, you see, and we haven't much money. And besides, why wear out shoes? Father says we ought to, though. Then father says me and Janet are both as wild as brumbies, and we ought to be our age. I suppose we are wild and all that, but we can take care of ourselves. Pompy, you see, knows judo. All the kids have learned it off him.'

Wearily she said she was just over eighteen, and then fell asleep with his arm still about her shoulders. The ants were bad, and the flies too. He brought the blanket roll from the pack-horse, and laid a blanket on hard clay-pan in the shadow and moved her to it. Then he sponged her face and sat beside her to prevent the flies from settling. He doubted she would have lived through the coming night. He wondered why no one had looked for her.

An hour later he was still keeping the flies at bay when three horsemen rode over the low ridge and down into the depression. Tony Carr was one of them. Another was large and hard, gimlet-eyed and stiff in the saddle. The third man was also large but not hard, and his eyes were frank. He rode loosely and with the ease of one used to horses all his life. They alighted, and the gimlet-eyed man advanced to stoop over the girl, listen to her breathing and lift the groundsheet to inspect her wounded foot. Straightening, his eyes widened. They were hazel and penetrating.

14

'Now, what's your name, and where d'you come from?' he demanded.

'Who are you?' returned Bony.

'Police,' snapped the big man.

'The name is Nat Bonnar. I've come down from Hall's Creek. I'm looking for horse work. I was on my way to Daybreak when I came across this young feller trying to make up his mind to cut the splinter from the girl's foot. We did that, and he went off to Daybreak for help.'

'What time did you get here?'

'Between four and five, I suppose.'

'You ought to get nearer than that. Your kind can generally tell the time by the sun. What was this young chap actually doing when you first saw him?'

'As I said, making his mind up about cutting a stick from the girl's foot.'

'When you got here, was she unconscious or asleep?'

'She was conscious. I heard her urging the young feller to cut the stick out.'

'And between you, you cut it out. Why didn't you pack the girl on one of the horses and bring her up to town?'

' 'Cos she was all in,' Carr replied for Bony, and was roughly told to shut up.

Tony's hands were clenched, but the policeman continued to stare at Bony, waiting for him to answer the question.

'The girl was exhausted by pain and exposure and thirst,' Bony said evenly, and continued: 'Also the golden rule is not to move an accident case until first examined by a medical expert.'

'Ah! Know-all, eh! When you first came in sight of this business, what was this young feller really doing?'

'He was kneeling beside the girl. He was looking at the stick protruding from the injured foot. In his right hand was a long, pointed knife. As it was obvious he wasn't going to cut the girl's throat, I tethered my horses, and knelt beside him. He said, in reply to the girl's urging: "I can't", and I said: "I can". We then proceeded to remove the stick.'

'You sure he wasn't interfering with her?'

15

'Interfering with her!' echoed Bony, his eyes masked. And the big man snapped:

'That's what I said. Come on. Out with it.'

'Nice clean mind you have,' Bony said and, indicating Tony, added: 'Looks all right to me. No black eyes. No bones broken.'

'Huh! We'll see what the girl says when she comes to. So you came from Hall's Creek, eh! What were you doing up there?'

'Breaking in a couple of colts for the policeman.'

'So. And the policeman's name?'

'Kennedy. Constable First-Class.'

'Oh! Soon check. I gotta horse you can break for me.'

He turned back to the girl, and Bony and Tony turned with him. The other man was bending over the girl, peering into her face, and on the girl's other side the dog was crouched with belly just clear of the ground, and lips lifted to reveal white fangs. The dog went to ground when the man straightened and said to the policeman:

'Sleeping all right. Musta had all it took. Lucky these two happened along.'

'Yes,' agreed the policeman. 'Coincidence. I don't like coincidences. No one comes down here ever, except you, Tony Carr, and you must explain just why you came this way this afternoon. And you too, whatever's your name. Blast! The stretcher party should be here by now.'

He strode away from them, proceeding to circle the place and examine the tracks left by horses and men, and must have seen the trail left by Joy Elder when crawling to the tree. It was then that the stretcher party appeared on the ridge, and he returned to meet them.

There were several men, two of them carrying the folded stretcher, and a young woman wearing blue slacks and a red jacket. As she came down to the floor of the depression, her walk bespoke the agility of youth. Bony estimated her age as well under thirty. Her hair was reddish-brown, and it glistened beneath the brim of the shallow straw hat.

Her interest was limited to the injured girl. They stood back watching her, noting that she felt the girl's pulse, then regarded the bandage about the wounded foot, without touching it. She spoke to the girl and, receiving no answer, raised an eyelid.

'All right, Bert Ellis, bring the stretcher. The blankets first, please, and one to cover her. Better take her to town. She'll need a little watching. You'll supervise, Mr Harmon?'

'Righto, Sister,' agreed the policeman.

Sister Jenks stood, nonchalantly produced a cigarette case, and removed a cigarette. A match was struck, and above the flame she looked into the masked blue eyes of Napoleon Bonaparte. She glanced away to the men engaged with the stretcher, protested at their work, and herself arranged the lifting of the inert girl to the stretcher and directed the manner of the covering. Bony was taking the now unwanted blanket roll to the pack-horse when he heard her call him. She wanted to know who he was. He told her.

'You removed the stick, I'm told.'

'Yes, Marm,' he replied, looking into her dark eyes, surveying the delicate features of the small face, not the least revealing being the determined chin.

'What did you do?'

He detailed the rough operation with the sterilized knife, the antiseptic and subsequent dressing.

'Sensible,' she voted. 'You couldn't have done better in the circumstances.'

'Thank you, Marm.'

'Oh, that's all right . . . Bonnar, I think you said? Don't call me Marm. I'm Sister Jenks, and I've never been married. May I be inquisitive for half a minute?'

'For ten minutes do you wish, Sister.'

'All right. See if you'll smile at my questions. Your mother was an aborigine?'

'I have been so informed,' Bony replied, smiling slightly.

'And your father was white?'

'That is additional information, Sister.'

'You are an oddity, Bonnar – a man of two races having adorable blue eyes. Are you not Inspector Napoleon Bonaparte?'

'Could be.'

17

'End of inquisitiveness, plus rudeness. No forgiveness asked. I am very glad you have come. We are not at all happy in Daybreak. You are working incognito?'

Bony nodded, saying:

'In this investigation a horsebreaker might succeed more quickly than a known detective.'

For the first time, Sister Jenks smiled, and Bony was obliged to keep pace with her.

'I hope to meet you again soon,' she said. 'I must tell you what my aunt says about you, just to see how vain you'll become. Now I must hurry after my patient. It's going to be fun knowing you. And I shall keep your secret.'

CHAPTER 3

The New Yardman

When Bony rode from the depression where grew the ghost gums, the men were loading the stretcher on to a utility stopped by rough ground half a mile up the long slope. The horsemen were riding to town on a more direct route.

Following the truck's trail, he came to a track rising diagonally towards the town, and falling away in the other direction to a distant clump of sandalwoods, amid which could be seen dwellings which he guessed comprised Dryblowers Flat. He passed the butcher's killing yards and skin shed, skirted the remains of Sam's Find, and so came to Main Street by the back door.

Main Street was wide and divided by thriving pepper trees, each being encircled by a wooden bench. Main Street! Why 'Main' could not be determined, as there were no side streets. The number of people on the unmade sidewalks tended to surprise, as did the several cars and utilities parked angle-wise. There was a small crowd outside the house where the truck which had brought in the wounded girl was parked. Now dismounted, the policeman, young Carr, and the third rider were talking outside the police station.

Bony rode carelessly by them. He found the one hotel at the far end of Main Street, which there abruptly became the track, rising and falling over the vast land swells, to the distant rail-head at Laverton.

The hotel was the last building on the west side of Main Street. A small and neat school of arts faced it from the opposite side. Between these buildings was a stone statue of a man for ever gazing towards Laverton, or ever waiting to welcome the traveller to Daybreak. He wore no hat. His hair was unruly, and his moustache was full and slightly drooping. The left arm hugged to his side a violin and bow, and in the right hand, held forward as though in greeting, was what looked like a nugget of gold. Chiselled expertly into the low stone base was inscribed:

MR SAMUEL LOADER

Bony surveyed the Hotel Melody Sam, a single-storeyed wood-built erection having a log front. There was no one outside and, as far as he could see and hear, no one inside. Every other place of business was fairly busy.

Nodding to the stone man, he rode his horses into the hotel yard, in the centre of which grew a gnarled and solitary gum tree. Bordering the yard were horse-yards, stables and sheds, and a row of five bachelor's bedrooms. He watered the horses and put them into an empty yard. No one was in view, and were it not for smoke issuing from a rear chimney the place could be thought deserted.

He entered the bar from the front, found it void of customers, discovered a compact woman seated on a high stool behind the counter and engrossed in a highly-coloured picture magazine.

'Evening!' she said, looking up. Her hair was jet-black and plastered to her head. Her face was red and polished like a gibber. A necklace of pearls first caught the eye, then the flash of diamonds on her hands.

'Evening!' politely countered Bony. 'Now a nice cool beer. Then a room, and the adjuncts.'

'Travelling, eh?'

'Travelling is correct, Marm.'

The woman made no move to draw or pour a nice cool beer. She said:

'No beer. All the beer's down under. So's Melody Sam. So's a case of gelignite and caps and fuse. You try to go down for beer, and we'll go up in flames and smoke.'

The woman pretended more interest in her paper than in her customer, and thoughtfully Bony rolled a cigarette and was smiling when he struck a match. This bar-room was spotless, airy and empty. The floor was polished and on it no smallest litter indicated any business. The framed pictures of unnatural horses were clean and level, and the bar counter was neat with its tray and glasses. Peace, when all should have been uproar.

'I think you said something about gelignite.'

'And about the fuse and detonators and such like,' agreed the woman, who could not be called a barmaid because, with the pearls, she was wearing a necklace of gold nuggets. 'Yes, that's how the beer is. All down below with Melody Sam. Haven't seen you before.'

'Staying for a while, if you'll fix me with a room. The name's Bonnar, Nat Bonnar.'

The woman left her stool, and peered at the page of an open book on the narrow bench at the back of the bar. Returning, she said:

'Number Seven. Dinner's at seven. Breakfast's at seven. It's all seven ... three of a kind.' Her dark eyes narrowed when she smiled, and when she smiled twenty odd years flew out of the door. He experienced the sensation of his face being explored, and he watched the expression in the dark eyes become one of warm interest when he held their gaze with his own. He knew precisely what was going on ... forgetfulness of his duality of race. She said:

'Sorry about the beer. He'll come up soon. Been down there now for eight days. Has these turns, you know.'

Bony chuckled, and the woman smiled again.

'All crossed tracks to me,' he confessed. 'I take it that Melody Sam is down in the cellar on a bender. And that he has explosives with him, which he will set off if anyone goes down after him, or the beer. That right?'

'Correct. He does it about twice a year. Sort of saves up for it. Plants a case of gelignite, and the doings, tin of kero and a lamp, and then without warning slips down there and swears he'll blow the place to bits if . . . As I said, if anyone goes down after him or more beer.'

'And you really believe he will blow the place up if . . .'

'I really think. Which is why I won't go down there, or allow anyone else to. You see, Melody Sam owns the hotel and all, and after he dies I own the hotel and all. So I'm not having the hotel blasted.'

'It would be a pity, with the nearest hotel a hundred and fifty miles away at Laverton,' agreed Bony, matching the woman's coolness. 'What does the local policeman say about it?'

'What can he? Law says we keep open to provide food and drink for man and beast. Well, we're open. We're not compelled by law to serve wine and spirits and beer. We serve food and tea or coffee to people, and we have hay and water for horses. As it is, there's plonk and spirits still on the shelves. The law don't say the licensee has to sell beer he owns, and if he likes swilling on his own property, and sitting on a case of gelignite, well, there's nothing in the law against that.'

'You could be right,' doubtfully agreed Bony.

'Oh, I know what I'm talking about.'

'But surely Melody Sam should be prevented from blowing the place to matchwood?'

'How?' contended the woman. 'Assuming I allowed it, who would take a chance and go down below? No one that I know. Even the policeman wouldn't take a chance. You wouldn't either, not after you see Melody Sam holding a lighted match to the end of a short piece of fuse. No one's game to go down, even if I agreed to it. No one's game to come in here and ask even for a nobbler of whisky. That's how it is, Bonnar. You staying?'

'If you can stand the tickling of anticipation to the soles of your feet, I can,' he said. 'Anyway, almost two hours yet to dinner, and I may as well stay here and keep you company.'

'Nice of you. Come far?'

'From the Creek.'

'Oh, quite a way.'

'How are you called?'

'Katherine Loader. Kat for short.' The gold nuggets about her throat reflected shafts of sunshine when she laughed. 'You're Nat Bonnar. Nat for short. Kat and Nat! Married?'

Bony's even white teeth gleamed, and his blue eyes momentarily sparkled, as each summed up the other for a second impression. He was of medium height and build, and there were springs in his legs and ropes in his arms resting on the counter. They possessed one attribute in common. Despite her black dress and tightly dressed hair, and the wealth about her neck and on her hands, and despite his rough riding clothes and drill shirt open at the neck, and sleeves rolled above the elbows, both had that well-groomed appearance which emanates from the spirit rather than the person. As she waited for his answer, he said:

'What d'you think?'

'I'd bet on it. I'm only lucky at cards.'

'That how you will own the pub one day?'

'No. I'm old Sam's granddaughter. And I'll never own the pub. He'll never die. He's just the same now as he was when I was a little girl. My father looked twice as old as Sam when he died at sixty. Hark at him down there!'

The voice was full yet sepulchral beneath the floorboards ... a pleasing baritone!

'Oh, come to me arms, me darlin'.'

Silence for a moment, then the accompaniment softly played on a violin:

'Oh, come to me arms, me darlin',
Oh, come to me arms right now!
Oh, tell me you love me, me darlin',
While I gurgle and guggle you down.'

Nat and Kat gazed at each other over the bar counter whilst

awaiting the next stanza, verse, or whatever. When there was but silence, relieved only by distant street noises, Bony said:

'Isn't there any more to it?'

'Don't think. He makes it up as he goes. You like a cup of tea?'

'I certainly would,' assented Bony promptly, and fell to rolling yet another cigarette when the woman left the bar by the passage door. A strange situation, was his verdict. The town full of people, and the only hotel full of emptiness. Unreasonable. Unheard of. Beyond his experience. It is said that Australia rides on the sheep's back. All tosh, of course, because it floats on beer. Yet he had entered this hotel and called for beer, and was offered tea! Someone at the open street doorway said:

'Old Sam still down under?'

Bony turned to see the little man Sister Jenks had named Ellis when arranging the stretcher.

'Could be,' he replied. 'Just heard the old boy singing.'

'Well, you gotta nerve, anyhow,' asserted Ellis.

'Why?'

'Standin' there as calm as you like. Don't you know Melody Sam always locks himself down under with a case or two of gelly, caps, fuse and all?'

'I have just been told so,' admitted Bony.

'Well ... Blimey! Runnin' a risk, ain't you? Makes me sick in me stommick, just hanging around here. You can have it.'

The little man vanished. Bony heard someone ask if the beer was still off, and Ellis's reply was akin to a moan of anguish. When Kat Loader returned with a tea tray, he said:

'You say your grandfather's been on a bender for eight days. Isn't it time he came up for air?'

'He's probably getting round to it. Milk and sugar in your tea?'

'Thank you, Miss ... Missus ...'

'Miss. Kat for short, like I said. Don't worry over Sam. He'll come to light some day.'

'What's he living on?'

23

'Nothing. The whisky's living on him.'

'But he can't go on long, surely?'

'Can't he! His top record so far is fifteen days, two years ago.' The woman chuckled, genuinely mirthful, and Bony thought she must be dead from the ears up, or the most placid woman he had ever encountered.

'Oh, come to me arms, me darlin'.'

Bony stamped a foot hard, and the singer stopped in his tracks. The woman's eyes opened wide, and her face paled. The vivacity in her stilled to marble.

'Oh, come to me . . .'

Again Bony stamped a foot, and this time shouted:

'Quiet, down there. Quiet, I say!'

A bow was scraped across taut strings. Silence filled with potential menace, then the singer's voice dispelled it.

'Hell's delight! Who's that up there telling me to be quiet?'

'Giggle,' whispered Nat to Kat. 'Make believe I'm an ardent lover. Go on.'

Reaching over the counter he gripped her wrist.

'Scuffle your feet on the floor,' he commanded.

He scuffled his own boots, and smiled happily when the woman actually did giggle, and he said loudly:

'Never mind about the old coot down below, love.'

'You stop it, Nat,' and proof was given that the woman was a born actress . . . as all women have been since Eve. 'No, not here, Nat. Not here, please.'

'Just one, Kat darlin',' pleaded Nat. More scuffling followed as they moved along the counter to the drop-flap, which already was open. Then a crash as the trap-door above the steps leading down to the cellar was flung up, and there emerged, as though from the grave, Melody Sam.

Standing clear of the trap, he glared at the two temporary lovers. He stood well over six feet. He stood straight and strong like a tree. He looked worse than terrible; he looked just plain horrible.

As Melody Sam advanced to the counter, his granddaughter slid to one side, and eventually was behind him and ran to the trap, which she closed swiftly and silently. With both hands supporting himself against the counter, the unwashed, be-whiskered, flaring-eyed monstrosity glared at Bony, who was calmly rolling a cigarette.

'What's your name, stranger?' he demanded.

'I'm Nat Bonnar.'

'What you doin' here, Mister Nat Bonnar?'

'I'm the new yardman,' he answered, lighting the cigarette. 'Didn't you know?'

'The new yardman!' roared the ancient immortal. 'Hey, Kat! What's this about a new yardman?'

Kat was rolling empty barrels over the trap-door. She said, and now her voice was shrill:

'I put him on just now. What about it?'

'What about it!' shouted the old man. 'Who's the flaming licensee around here?' He lurched to the open cut in the counter and advanced upon Bony. 'Out you go, whatever your name is. I do the hiring in this place, and I do the firin' too. I'm the boss of this pub. I'm the boss of this town as well. You going peaceful?'

'I'm not going at all,' whined Nat Bonnar. 'I don't know you. Never seen you before. The lady here put me on as yardman, and yardman I'm goin' to be until she sacks me. Now you keep off me. You touch me, and I'll have the Union sue you, see? I'm a workin' man, and we have our rights.'

Melody Sam exploded. A vast shout of laughter rocked him on his bare feet, and blew a hurricane through his forest of whiskers.

'Bash me ribs! The feller tells me he has rights,' he roared. 'Rights! Rights, he says! Now, Mister Working Man who has rights, I got the rights to heave you out of my pub, and when you stop going it will be against the garage on the other side of the track.'

The granddaughter was adding an ice-chest to the barrels on the cellar trap, and her back was towards the couple in the middle of the bar-room. She heard a short, smart slap, and turned in time to see her ancestor swaying groggily on his feet and then collapse into the arms of Nat Bonnar.

'You hit him!' she cried.

'He fell asleep on his two feet,' indignantly countered Bony, and hauled the body over a shoulder. 'A good yardman can do much about a place like this. Besides cleaning up the yard and tossing out the drunks, helping in the bar and carting away the empties, he can be a wonderful companion to the boss. Where shall I dump your grandfather?'

'This way,' replied the granddaughter. 'No, wait. Hold him.' She almost ran to the front door and slammed it shut and bolted it. Then she ran out through the door to the passage, and Bony heard her shut and lock the main house door. When she appeared at the passage door, she beckoned, calling: 'This way. I'll show you the Lion's Den we always put him in.'

The burdened Bony staggered after her. They passed through the kitchen, watched with amazement by the cook and a housemaid. Then out into the yard, and, turning right, came to an outbuilding which had bars to its small high window, and a door so thick a horse could not have kicked it open. Within was a bunk and blankets placed for a lodger.

'Put him there,' ordered Kat Loader.

Bony laid out the body, and the woman drew up the blankets. The body moaned, and the eyelids deep in the forest of whiskers trembled.

'He'll come to in a minute. Let's leave him, quick.'

She almost pushed Bony out of this strong-room, which even had a small opening in the massive door, protected by two iron bars. She shot a bolt, and turned the key in a padlock, and she was panting a little and trembling slightly. Her voice suddenly was a little frightened, and as suddenly was firm again.

'They know already,' she said. 'Listen!'

Beyond the yard fence the street was alive. Men shouted. Others whistled. And more were pounding on the hotel doors.

'Come on,' ordered the granddaughter of Melody Sam. 'Into the bar before they break in the doors.'

Taking hold of Bony's hand, she literally dragged him into the kitchen, through it to the passage and along to the bar, calling to the cook to follow. The pounding at the front door

26

was urgent. Men peering through the windows shouted and set up a cheer.

'Shift all that stuff off the trap,' ordered the woman. 'Quick about it, now. That's right. Now, Nat, down you go and haul up the bottled beer for a start. And, Sue, you take it from Nat and open the cases and set out the bottles to serve.'

'I'm to be the new yardman?' queried Nat Bonnar. 'True?'

'You are the new yardman, Nat,' she told him, holding open the trap-door, and revealing the flight of steps down to the floor of the cellar, where burned a kerosene lamp near a large case on which was a length of fuse and a box of detonators. 'Be quick, Nat, before they break something. Of course you are the yardman. You're going to be the loveliest yardman we ever had at Daybreak.'

And Detective-Inspector Napoleon Bonaparte proceeded to re-float Australia on beer.

CHAPTER 4

The Magnifying Glass

There was a period, seemingly very short, when Joy Elder floated from one place to another, and at each place paused only to choose the biggest garnet of those lying as thickly as the mica specks on the slopes away up from Dryblowers Flat. Then she was conscious that she was actually awake, that she felt drowsy, and that pain rhythmically thudded against her body. Now she remembered. She was lying with her back against a ghost gum, and Tony Carr and a strange man were crouched over her foot. She remembered how Tony had looked at her, an expression of sick horror in his eyes, and how the other man was looking at her foot and doing something with a tin pannikin filled with blood, or red stuff, anyway.

That was a long time ago. The sun had gone and it was night, and the moon was in the sky, masked by dust haze, its light dim

27

and brown. Tony Carr was no longer there. He must have gone for help. The other man was there, though. She felt rather than saw him crouched beside her. His eyes were strangely blue and filled with compassion, and there had never been anyone just like him. He was holding her hand and his fingers were gently stroking her wrist and making her think of her mother, who had died so long ago down in Kal.

Somewhere a clock was ticking, and there couldn't be a ticking clock here in the depression where the ghost gums lived. Funny! There were no stars up there; only a white roof, a ceiling. She was inside a house. She was in bed, between sheets. And the strange man was sitting beside her, and still caressing her wrist.

'Where am I?' she asked plaintively, because the foot was aching like a burn.

'In Sister Jenks's little hospital,' replied Bony. 'Can I get you anything?'

'Please, a drink. I'm so thirsty. I could drink and drink. I've never been so thirsty before.'

'Perhaps we could persuade Sister to make us a cup of tea. How would that do?'

'Two cups, please. Three cups.'

She watched him move towards the end of the room. There was light there and she could see three other beds that seemed to be vacant. She heard him call softly for Sister Jenks, and at once the sister replied: 'What is it? Who is that?'

'The patient is awake and asking for a drink. Perhaps a pot of tea ... perhaps two pots of tea, Sister.' Bony replied, and came back to sit again beside Joy's bed. To Joy Elder he whispered: 'Now I am going to be nagged at for being here. Don't you say anything.'

Arrayed in a floral gown, carrying an oil lamp, Sister Jenks appeared. She placed the lamp on a table near the door, and came forward to stand at the foot of the bed, to be halted by amazement.

'What on earth are you doing here, Nat Bonnar?'

'Just watching the patient, Sister. Couldn't sleep, so thought I'd come along and sit with her. She's awake.'

28

'So I can see,' agreed Sister Jenks, and bent over Joy and asked how she felt.

'My foot hurts, Sister, and I'm so thirsty.'

'All right, dear, we'll see to it. Nat Bonnar, first door to the right is the kitchen. Go make a pot of strong tea. And stay there till I come.'

There was a pressure lamp on the kitchen bench, which Bony quickly had in action. There was also a pressure stove, on which he soon had water heating. He found a teapot and a caddy of tea, and located the ice-chest for the milk. The tea was brewing when Sister Jenks came in from her patient. Her small features were hardened by anger, and her eyes sparkled.

'Now, Nat Bonnar, alias So-and-So, what's the meaning of this?'

'Hush! A nice cup of tea for the patient, and perhaps a bite to eat. Tea for ourselves, and then, Sister, the upbraiding.'

'Well, your effrontery leaves me gasping,' she almost hissed. 'How did you break your way into the ward?'

'I didn't break in,' countered Bony, pouring tea into the cups, and holding the pot so high that splashes fell on the clean white cloth he had found. 'Breaking and entering is a serious offence in law. Just walking in is much less so. So I just walked in ... through the back doorway, the door being unbolted.'

'You didn't. I bolted that door last thing.'

'Meanwhile the patient suffers thirst,' Bony mildly pointed out. 'A cup of tea right now, with a couple of thin slices of bread and butter. Followed in an hour with a good hearty meal of tough steak and week-old bread. She'll be so bucked she will be able to run all the way to Dryblowers Flat.'

'What nonsense!' expostulated Sister Jenks, and took the small tray he held to her. She marched to the door and knew she looked a trifle ridiculous, and felt like dropping the tray and ... and ...

Nat Bonnar drew a chair to the table and thankfully enjoyed the tea and bread and butter. Five minutes, and Sister Jenks returned and sat with him, glared at him, then snapped:

'At least you owe me an explanation.'

'I do,' he agreed. 'Now is the time for it. There is

always a time for everything. First what do you think of that girl?'

'Her condition? Temperature is up. The wound is inflamed, and that's your fault. The potash solution you used to wash out the wound was much too strong. You ought to have known better.'

'But you didn't operate with a butcher's knife and see the wound as I saw it. You didn't see the dirt and the blow-fly grubs, and you don't take into account that mulga wood is poisonous and that the wound was more than twenty-four hours old when I had to deal with it. And, further, you don't give credit for the fact that I am an itinerant bush worker, not a doctor, or hospital-trained as you are.'

'How like you are to what I've been told!' she said with conviction. 'We'll leave it. What are you doing in here at four in the morning?'

'Are we friends or enemies?'

'What a man! Answer my question.'

'What a woman! You answer mine.'

Sister Jenks returned to the chair she had vacated.

'Did my aunt or my uncle tell you about me?' she asked.

'Your uncle did invite me to dinner five days ago,' he conceded. 'We talked of many things, including you and your work at Daybreak.'

'Then we must be friends.'

'There is no compulsion,' he pointed out.

Their eyes clashed across the table. She said:

'No, there is no compulsion. Forgive me for being irritable. My mental pictures of you have proved blurred. Patient's soup will be ready. You'll stay?'

Bony nodded and the slight figure in the flowered gown passed to the stove to serve the meal for the patient. She was absent for half an hour, saying, on returning:

'Almost asleep. She'll do for a few hours. I don't like the foot, though. And I'm sure I bolted that door.'

'It was not only unbolted. It was ajar.'

'And you believe someone crept in here while I was asleep?'

30

Bony shrugged, and lit another cigarette from the small pile he had made while she was with the patient.

'I've got myself a job at the hotel as yardman,' he announced. 'After the beer drought, the bar was kept open till midnight. I was prospecting Main Street, and thought I saw a man enter your side gate. A late hour for a visit when your house was in darkness. I came along to check. The front door was secure. The windows hadn't been tampered with. The back door was ajar. I came in, closed the back door and bolted it, and sat with the patient until she woke. At what time did you lie down to sleep?'

'Half past ten. The clock woke me at half past twelve to visit the patient. She was asleep then, as I thought she would be, with the tablet I'd given her. Then I went back to bed.'

'You didn't go outside via the back door?'

'No. And I didn't go to the back porch for anything, so didn't notice the door being open. I'm certain I bolted the door before lying down at ten-thirty. We have a murderer in Daybreak, you know!'

'Then the door was opened by someone between ten-thirty and five minutes to one, when I came in.'

'But why? For what reason?' pressed Sister Jenks.

'There are always countless "whys" associated with an investigation. May I suggest that you retire to your room and sleep again? I'll sit here and ponder on the probable answers to the "whys".'

'Sleep, Nat! May I call you Nat?'

'It would be safer to confine yourself to Nat.'

'I couldn't sleep, not now. That tea is cold. I'll brew another pot. Something to eat? Cold meat and bread and butter?'

When he accepted, she turned once again to the bench, halted and said. 'Supposing that man came in just before you did. He might be still inside the house.'

'Be assured that he isn't. I've sniffed into every room, including yours.'

'Sniffed into every room!' she echoed, and he chuckled with delight.

'Sniffed, it was. Merely stood just inside every room and

31

sniffed. Like the witch-doctors of Africa, and some in Australia, I can sniff out an enemy. I found your antiseptics a little distracting to my nose, but I'm confident that my nose didn't let me down.'

'And you sniffed into my room, too?'

'Yes.'

'Well, of all the nerve!'

'I had to ... to be assured that no male prowler was in your room.'

'Oh! Well, I give up, Nat.'

'As well in the beginning as later. And you don't want to sleep?'

'No. I want to ask you some questions.'

'How extraordinary,' he exclaimed, mockingly. 'I want to ask you some questions. Permit me, selfishly, to be first. On arriving here with the girl, what followed? Who brought her in?'

'Bert Ellis and Bob Merke. Bert works for the Town Council and Merke with his brother in the only garage we have.'

'They carried her into the ward, I suppose?'

'Yes.'

'And left immediately?'

'Yes. Just before they did, the girl's sister, Janet, appeared. She's two years older than Joy. They both live with their father at Dryblowers Flat, and, like all of them down there, the sisters are, shall I say, a little difficult to understand. Anyway, Janet was perfectly cool about her sister. She helped me undress her and put her into bed, and she made no fuss over assisting me to attend to the foot, which, as you know, wasn't pretty to look at. A Mrs Powell who comes in to housekeep for me prepared food, and we roused the girl to take nourishment.'

'Just you three women and the patient. Anyone call?'

'Harmon, the policeman, came. He wanted to question the patient, but I said he'd have to wait until the morning.'

'No one else?'

'No. Of course there was a good deal of talk about it outside. When Janet left she was questioned plenty by the townsfolk. Her father was there, but she pacified him.'

'Was Janet wearing shoes, d'you remember?'

'No. She must have come from Dryblowers without waiting to change into her town clothes.'

'Your housekeeper ... she left before you locked the back door for the night?'

'Oh yes. You are worried about that door, aren't you?'

Bony smiled, and rolled a cigarette, or what might be called one. He said:

'Your aunt informed me that you have been wasting your fresh young life for three years by working among these awful bush people, and that she wished you were working in a city hospital where you would meet so many nice young doctors. Now, now! Her words, not mine. I defended you and the awful bush people. I refer to your work and the period you have spent at Daybreak only to register two facts. One, that you know every man, woman and child, and two, that you were here before the series of crimes began. Is it true that the first of these crimes occurred after Antony Carr came to Daybreak?'

'Yes. He had been here about five months when the aboriginal was killed. But I cannot believe ...'

'Believe nothing of any person in this situation we have at Daybreak. It is pre-conceived ideas and unfounded opinions that have contributed to the creation of confusion. All born in the minds of people whose interests in life are extremely limited.'

'And you think my interests in life are extremely limited?'

Across the table the dark eyes gleamed, and the shapely mouth matched the determined chin. Slowly Bony smiled.

'I think it likely. Your aunt is sure of it. Now if we could tell her that your base doctor is young and handsome and unmarried, you see how extended your interests in life could become.'

'All Aunt thinks about is having me married, Nat.'

The expression of pique vanished, and Sister Jenks smiled in a manner belying her youth. 'Now what is all this leading to?'

'The disclosure of the person responsible for three murders at Daybreak, all within six months. You know that person. You

33

knew the three victims. You are, I hope, the magnifying-glass I shall use to examine them and all others living in and about Daybreak. A little badinage and a little teasing are the cloths with which to polish the glass.'

'Then I hope you won't use the magnifying-glass to examine me,' she said, and he countered with:

'I have already employed my own glass to do that, Sister Jenks.'

CHAPTER 5

Introduction to Daybreak

Main Street delighted Bony, for the roadway, divided by the thriving pepper trees, was unsurfaced, and the sidewalks were unpaved. As he crossed the street to the police compound, he noted with satisfaction the man recorded as council staff methodically sweeping into heaps tree débris and litter, and others were sweeping outside their shops and houses their section of sidewalk. Every morning, therefore, Main Street would be nicely prepared to receive the imprints of human feet.

The police compound was spacious and, of course, orderly. There was the detached office and the policeman's house on the right, the cell block of four lockups behind the house, the stables and sheds and horse yard on the opposite side. There was enough spare room to drill a troop of mounted men.

Obeying a shout from Constable Harmon, Bony entered the office.

'Sit down,' the constable ordered, pointing to the chair opposite his desk. 'Been checking up on you. Found you OK with Hall's Creek. That right, you've taken the job as yardman over at the pub?'

Nat Bonnar, the bush horsebreaker, self-consciously shuffled his feet, and probed into pockets for the makings. After hesitation, he raised his gaze to meet that of the policeman, and

34

Harmon decided that the clash of eyes the previous day must have been the result of excitement in this otherwise normal bush worker.

'You can smoke if you want,' he said.

'Thanks. Yes, I took the job on at the pub. Had to trick old Melody Sam up from his booze-hole. He's pretty sick this morning.'

'I saw him,' grunted the policeman. 'What I been thinking, Nat, is that you might do a job for me. Private job. I got a horse, a gelding, three-year-old, bit of an outlaw, but has all it takes. Too good for me to tackle, and my tracker isn't up to par, there. Would you take him on?'

'Break him in to saddle?'

'That's it. I like horses, good horses. That gelding's a bastard, but I like him, too.'

'All right, I'll look him over,' Bony drawled. 'Could work him in my spare time, you arrange it with Miss Loader.'

'I'll do that. She's not difficult. Besides, you do a good job on him and I won't be mean. Anyway, I'll have him brought to the yard this afternoon, and we can talk it over then. Melody Sam still locked inside the Lion's Den?'

'Was, half an hour ago. What is that place?'

Harmon chuckled. 'Old Melody Sam built the pub in the Year One, and he built that outside place as a lockup because there wasn't one here, or a policeman, either. Now it's used to lock him up. You looking after him? How are you treating him for the ding-bats?'

'He gets one teaspoon of whisky to one pint of soup. Has to drink half a gallon of soup to get the effect of the whisky, and that isn't much of an effect, either. He's like the grey gelding you been telling about ... pretty wild.' Bony stood, and Harmon waved him back to the chair.

'Your horse, Mr Harmon. Wasn't he broken properly in the first place?'

Strange how a man can be dominated by a horse. The man ruled by a woman or gripped by the gambling fever, the drug-addict and the slave of John Barleycorn, all are comparatively free men. To Bony, Constable Harmon had been a nasty suspicious policeman; now a grey horse changed him to a hail-fellow-well-met type of character and, without doubt, while a horse occupied his mind he was bearable. So they talked horses, the one admitting that the wayward gelding was too good for him, and the other outlining the training necessary for this paragon of a horse.

For the second time Bony rose, and again was waved back.

'Seems to me, Nat, we could get along,' Harmon said, and Bony was aware that he was going to change the subject. 'Fact is, my tracker isn't up to scratch. Abos in this country are still pretty wild, and when a tracker is wanted most times they're away out beyond, on walkabout or something. You heard about the murders, I suppose?'

'Not much,' admitted Nat. 'Seems a clever feller.'

'Just plain cunning, Nat. You know, we could use you if another murder happens. Kennedy up at Hall's Creek gives you a pretty good reputation. Being yardman and barman, you might pick up a lead. You never know. The feller who did those murders is still walking about Daybreak. I'm sure of it. I know him. We all know him.'

'But not as the murderer,' amended Bony.

'As you say, Nat. What we're up against is a lack of clues and no leads; at least nothing much to boast about. The first murder was done at the end of Main Street and right outside the Manse. Young abo girl. Supposed to be working at the Manse. Anyway, the parson's wife was looking after her, teaching her to speak our language and to be useful in the house. Slept in a bed . . . education got as far as that . . . and was found next morning fully dressed and her head clubbed in.

'Early the day before, the tribe had gone on walkabout, my tracker with 'em. There was a bit of trouble in the tribe over the girl, and I thought it was a tribal killing, one of the bucks being sent back to carry it through. Body on soft ground, but no abo tracks; you know how they can wipe their own tracks out.

'When the second murder happened I changed my mind about the first being an abo one. Five miles out on the road to Laverton is a homestead owned by a man named Lorelli. He's in town late one day, and on getting home he finds his wife in the kitchen, strangled. All about the place were tracks of a man wearing ordinary sandshoes size eight, weighing about a hundred and sixty, and having a slight limp in the right leg. And the abos away again on walkabout, and me with no tracker.

'Some of us here ain't new chums on tracking, Nat, but the bloke got away by hopping over surface rocks, and the Laverton policeman couldn't locate a tracker for two days, and he got no further. Windy weather, too.'

'No one working for Lorelli?' interjected Bony, assuming ignorance.

'The hired man was down on a spell to Kalgoorlie. I made plaster casts of the tracks we found there. And that was all we got. Happened last August. And then, blow me down if a young lad who worked at the garage and lived at Dryblowers Flat, and rode to and from work on a bike, didn't have his throat cut, right close to the mine. And the tracks of the feller wearing sandshoes all about the body. And, Nat, the abos away on walkabout again, my tracker and all.'

'No doubt about it being the same man?'

'Took plaster casts. They were compared by experts with the first set. No doubt, Nat.'

'Doesn't add up, Mr Harmon.'

'As you say,' sombrely agreed the policeman. 'No motive. No background of quarrels, fights, anything. You know, Nat, I been wondering. I took a spare of those plaster casts, and if I made prints with them, d'you think you'd remember if you happened to see that feller's tracks when he was wearing boots? Could you tell us more about him than the Laverton tracker and the feller they brought up from Kalgoorlie? Think you could?'

'Well, I could try,' conceded Bony. 'Think he'll murder someone else?'

'Bound to,' asserted Harmon. 'They never stop once they start. Yes, we'll give it a go one day, Nat. Meanwhile you handle the grey and let us know what you think of him. I'll fix it with Kat Loader, and Melody Sam, when he's fit to be loosed.'

'All right, Mr Harmon.'

'And nothing about working with me on the murders, Nat. That's between us. I'll look after you, you play along with me, eh?'

Bony agreed, and this time was permitted to stand. On how many occasions had he sought cooperation from a bush policeman and received it? This was the first time a bush policeman had sought his cooperation.

On coming to the office he had distinctly seen a face behind the grille of one of the cells. Now the door of that cell was wide open. Turning back to the office, he said:

'Thought you had a sardine in the tin, Mr Harmon. Seems like he slipped out.'

Harmon's face beetrooted. He strode from the office, stared at the cell block, and swore with artistry.

'Damn! Drunk and disorderly last night. I put him in. The beak gave him three days this morning. Now he's out, and I want them stables repaired. Blast!'

Bony watched the large man striding from the yard to the street so prominently located by the great pepper trees spaced along the centre. Then he noted the woman sweeping the veranda of the station house, and when she saw him, she beckoned, and he went to the veranda edge and looked up at her, as the veranda itself was two feet above the ground.

'Are you Nat Bonnar?' she asked. She was small and yet wiry, and when she moved she dragged her left leg. Suffering had added falseness to her age, and beauty to her dark eyes. Bony smiled up at her, and a lightness displaced the sadness on her face.

'Yes, I'm Nat Bonnar,' he replied. 'And who are you?'

'I'm his sister. I'm Esther Harmon. I let the prisoner free.'

A smile, the ghost of a tiny smile, crept about her mouth.

'You let the prisoner out!' echoed Bony. 'The policeman's sister! Why?'

'Oh, I suppose because George is too strict. You see, Ed McKay's all right. He got drunk last night after the drought, and George collared him and locked him up. Then the magistrate gave him three days this morning, and I know George got him the three days because he wants repairs done to the stables.

38

It's hot inside those cells, and poor Ed McKay was worried about his cows, his wife being poorly and no one to milk them. So I let him out to milk the poor things.'

Inspector Bonaparte was rarely nonplussed.

'Now your brother has to find him, and bring him in again,' he said. 'D'you often let the prisoners out?'

'No. It depends. You see, everyone knows everyone else in Daybreak. It's such a small place. A woman has to have her fun sometimes. People have to be stirred up. Besides, Ed McKay's wife can't have him in a lockup when their cows need to be milked.'

'Perhaps not,' agreed Bony. 'Anyway, McKay can't have got far.'

'Oh no, he'll only be down at his cow-sheds.'

Two figures appeared in the street beyond the yard's open double gates, and Esther Harmon said:

'Trust misplaced. Ed wasn't milking his cows. He was over at the hotel drinking again.'

The men entered the yard, the policeman huge beside the wisp of a man who was obliged to take two steps to each one taken by the Law. The little man was coatless, and his feet were minus boots. The shock of grey hair was disturbed by the movement of his body, and he was complaining at being given the bum's rush back to the sardine tin. A man passed along the sidewalk beyond the gates and evinced no interest in this incident, and, having thrown the prisoner into the dungeon, Constable Harmon shot the bolts and returned to his office without speaking to his sister.

'I'll never trust that Ed McKay again,' sighed Miss Harmon. 'Men! They're all liars. They keeping old Melody Sam locked up over there?'

'Until he's fit,' Bony replied. 'He's comfortable enough.'

'How that granddaughter of his puts up with him I don't know. How we all put up with him I don't know either,' remarked Miss Harmon, and went on with her sweeping unembarrassed by her crippled leg. 'Just a nasty old bully, I think. Told him so more than once. You heard about our murders, I suppose?'

39

'Yes, a little. Three, weren't there?'

'Three, with three or four more to come. Give us something to talk about. They don't say, but they all think Tony Carr did it . . . all three. Blind as bats, everyone here is. You found Tony Carr with that ragamuffin Elder girl, didn't you? Think he could have strangled the lubra, and attacked the stockman's wife and killed the boy? Think he could?'

'He's strong enough, Miss Harmon.'

Her dark eyes gleamed like specks of new-won coal, and she leaned on the broom and glowered at him. She said:

'Yes, he's strong enough. Wish I could be sure about him. I wish . . . Oh, go away and leave me to my chores.'

The leg swung outward in an arc as she turned her back to him and went on with her sweeping, and he said:

'I'd like to talk with you again some time, Miss Harmon.'

She made no reply to that, and when he reached the street and glanced back she was still sweeping, although standing on the same place.

CHAPTER 6

Youth Without Armour

A famous doctor once declared that a man lived as long as his stomach, going so far as to add that a man is merely a stomach. He found that among the genuine bush workers a very high proportion lived to a great age, and he attributed this incidence of longevity to the bushman's imbalance of stomach intake: living for forty-eight weeks of the year on tea and alkali-loaded surface water, and the remaining four weeks on whisky. Thus every year the heavy stomach lining of tannin was removed by alcohol, and the stomach was entirely renovated.

Melody Sam's stomach apparently thrived on two benders a year, and in between he never drank anything but strong tea. On the occasion of Bony's visit, convalescence did not extend beyond three days, following which he attended to normal business, and when asked to join in a round, poured himself a nip from a whisky bottle filled with tea of the correct deceptive colour.

Bony did duty behind the bar counter longer than could be expected of a detective-inspector, but he really enjoyed the work, and it did bring him into friendly contact with nearly everyone at Daybreak. There was the council staff, a lanky, tired, ever-thirsty man named Bert Ellis. He comprised the staff of the Town Council, Melody Sam being the Town Council, plus the Town Engineer, Town Clerk, etc., etc. Then there was Leslie Thurley. Justice of the Peace, etc., etc., in addition to being the postmaster. He was ageing sixty, and his weak blue eyes peered from behind very strong lenses. His hardest cross was his wife. Fred Joyce, the butcher, was middle-aged, large and inclined to flabbiness. He had the face of an Irish tenor, and lost much through the absence of a brogue. There were many lesser lights illumining Daybreak society, and the dryblowers living at Dryblowers Flat had all been poured into the same mould.

The topics of conversation ranged from Constable Harmon's grey gelding to the current world tour now being enjoyed by the current State Premier and his wife and secretary, etc., etc. In between expressions of hope for the horse and damnation of the Premier, the subjects of local murders, gold and tin, and Tony Carr were decidedly popular.

On the day Joy Elder was permitted by Sister Jenks to return to her father's abode at Dryblowers Flat, Bony was given the opportunity of talking with Tony in less dramatic circumstances than on the first occasion. He had been exercising the gelding, and seeing young Carr, herding three beasts into the butcher's slaughter-yard, he tethered the horse to a post at Sam's Find, and sat in the shadow of the old poppet head, aware that the cattle would not be killed until sundown.

It was mid-afternoon in early April, when the sun is hot on face and arms, and the flies still a nuisance, to be kept at bay with a sprig of bush. The slopes of Bulow's Range were ablaze with fields of mica specks reflecting the sunlight, and away to

41

the west the mulga forest was a vast area of jade-green pile with never a moth blemish. The track passing Sam's Find sloped gently to skirt the butcher's yards and flow on down to the distant settlement of Dryblowers Flat, shaded by the sandal-woods of gleaming light-green in a world of salmon-pink, russet-brown, and spinifex silver-grey. Now and then the east-erly wind from the great Interior desert lands brought with it the magically blended perfume of the Fleeting Moment, and the Ageless Past.

As Tony Carr rode towards Sam's Find, Bony watched, and read the picture of a city youth not yet fully initiated. The hack he rode was old and lazy. The boy wore the bushman's clothes of tight trousers tucked into short leggings. He wore spurs, but wasn't game to use them. He carried a stock-whip, and had practised with it when driving the cattle, but had never hit a beast, and made a poor showing with its green silk cracker. There was the promise of the man. The sun and the wind had wiped clean from his face the pasty overlay of the city.

'Day, Nat!' he greeted Bony, and attempted to squat on his spurred heels, surrendered to inexperience, and finally sat on the ground, drawing his knees to his chin and moodily gazing into space.

'Day, Tony. You killing tonight?'

'Two beasts and six hoggets. How's the gelding shaping?'

'Coming along well.'

Constable Harmon's horse whinnied to Tony's ageing mare, and stamped its impatience on being also neckroped to a post.

'Not the outlaw everyone made out,' Bony drawled. 'Very few of 'em are.'

'Could be more human outlaws than horses,' sneered the boy.

'Could be! There are, Tony. What's worrying you?'

'Nothing. When you leave here, where'll you make for?'

'Haven't decided. Why?'

'Oh, nothin'. Look, why don't they give a feller a chance? I was over at Dryblowers after the cattle, and I met old Peter Gunther and his mate dryblowin', and I just said "Goodday",

42

and Peter hollers out telling me to get to hell away from Dryblowers Flat. I ain't got smallpox, have I?'

'Not smallpox, Tony; a record.'

'Yair, a record, and no one's ever goin' to forget it. Chipped by ole Harmon about finding Joy Elder, like I had half killed her, and was gonna to if you hadn't come by. Most of 'em blamin' me for the murders around here. A bit ago, I was out on the road to Lav and I came on old MacBride the parson stuck up with his car. He'd gone specking for gold, and somehow he had lost the ignition key, and when I crossed the wires for him in a couple of seconds and started the engine, he said I ought to give over starting cars like a young criminal pinching one. And after I'd saved him a four-mile walk!'

'As you resent the minister's comment, Tony, you should give up your criminal habits.'

The boy turned over on his side, the better to glare upward at Bony.

'I ain't done nothin' since I been here in Daybreak. Not a bloody thing,' he exploded. 'I like this place. I like some of the people. The boss treats me fair enough, and there's plenty to keep goin' with. The flamin' blacks are more friendly. They don't tell me to get away from 'em and they don't look at me like I done them murders.'

'Your boss is sponsor for you, isn't he?' questioned Bony.

'Yair. He's all right. Old Melody's fair enough too. They was gonna arrest me for the murders, but he stopped 'em. Said he'd pawn his pub and hire the best fronts in Australia to defend me if they did.'

'Oh! Why were they going to arrest you?' asked the surprised Bony, for this was a news item for him.

'Well, the day Mrs Lorelli was killed ... you heard about that, I suppose?' Bony nodded. 'Well, her old man was in town that day. He'd sold some hides to the boss and went on the booze with the dough. I didn't know about this at the time 'cos I was away down south bringing home a mob of steers the boss had bought off Wintarrie. I got to Lorelli's place just before sundown, and I was dry, as I'd forgot to fill me water-bag. So I went to their house tank and got a drink of water, and then went

43

on after the cattle and got 'em to the town common gate just before dark.'

'You didn't see Mrs Lorelli?'

'Yes, I did. They got a bit of a garden out there, and she was doing something in it, and just waved, and I waved back, as I couldn't leave the cattle too long.'

'Then, when her husband reached home about nine o'clock, he found her in the kitchen choked to death?'

'Yair. But I didn't do it. Harmon's tracker said so . . . when old Melody yelled at him. The tracker said a bloke wearin' sandshoes went there and done the job after I was there.'

'You never wear sandshoes?'

'No.'

'Some do in Daybreak, I suppose?'

'Them that plays tennis.'

'The store sells tennis shoes?'

'Expect so. They sells most things.'

'How did you come to injure your right leg?' The boy's hazel eyes were hard with abrupt suspicion, and he said:

'What d'you know about me leg?'

'You walk with a slight limp, Tony.'

'Well, I fell off a' roof one night and sort of tore something. Why?'

'That was, when? Before you came to Daybreak?'

Tony grinned. 'Yair. I was getting outer school. I fell off the roof instead of twisting over properly to drop from the guttering.'

'Then there was a boy killed about here, wasn't there? Going home to Dryblowers on his bike one night and was stopped by the feller wearing sandshoes.'

'Tom Moss, that was. Worked at the garage. Worked late that night on a rush job with a truck. No one said I did that, but a lot of 'em thought I did. Why would I? You tell me. He was in me hair, but not that crook that I'd bump him.'

'Mrs Lorelli wasn't killed for gain, either, was she?'

'No, don't think so.'

'What about the lubra, Mary, who worked for Mrs Mac-Bride and the minister?' prompted Bony with seeming

44

indifference. Carr did not respond at once.

'She got hers in the middle of the night right outside the Manse gate. Got woodened with something wot wasn't a bike chain.'

'How well did you know her? Was she young or old?'

'Youngish, I s'pose. About as old as Janet Elder. Hi! what's the idea? How much did I know her? Think I was runnin' around with her?'

Anger flared in the hazel eyes, fierce and eruptive. He swung his body over, raised himself to his knees and glared at Bony.

'Go easy,' urged Bony. 'I was only trying to get a picture of her. Why the fire? Go easy, Tony. Anyone would think I was accusing you of murdering her.'

'Well, I don't know nothin'. Let's talk about something else.'

It was the time to dig, and Bony said:

'Then tell me why you entered Sister Jenks's house that night Joy Elder was in the hospital ward.'

'I didn't . . .' On his knees, Carr moved close to the questioner. 'How did you know?' he asked, his eyes blank of expression.

'Your tracks outside the back door are how I know. The door was bolted on the inside. You managed to draw the bolt from the outside. Then when you were in the house something happened to make you fade quick, and you didn't have time, or forgot, to shut the door.'

'Yair. I'm slippin', Nat. I forgot to shut that flamin' door.'

'Why did you go in at that time of night?'

'Just wanted to see how the girl was.'

'Couldn't you have knocked at the front door earlier and asked Sister Jenks?'

'No. I asked her 'fore dinner, and she said sort of snappy that Joy was as good as could be expected. I don't hear no more. The boss told me next day she was doing all right. Anyhow what were you doing at the back door?'

'Sister Jenks didn't want to make a song and dance about the door being open after she had locked it the night before, and so asked me what I thought.'

'And you told her it was me?'

45

'Be your age, Tony.'

It was like watching the moon come from behind a cloud. The scowl gradually waned, and the smile which followed was halted by reluctant belief.

'You didn't say? True?'

'Why should I? You didn't do any harm. Very silly, though. Sister could have caught you.'

'Not me. I know me way around.'

Bony watched the boy, who was now sitting again with his knees drawn to his chin, and staring at that horizon no higher than his boot-tops.

'Joy has a sister called Janet, hasn't she? Good sports?'

'None of 'em's good sports to me, Nat. Got a record, I have. They're frightened of me, and old MacBride made 'em scared, see? Won't even speak. At least not before that time I found Joy with a crook foot. After that, this morning it was, Janet did give a "thank you", and she did tell me Joy was gettin' better fast.'

'Seems to me you've been kicked around.'

'I can take it. And I can dish it out, too.'

'Forget it, Tony. How do you get along with the blacks? Someone told me you go away with them sometimes, hunting and all that.'

'That's right. Lot of 'em are decent blokes in their own way. I met up with a coupla young fellers soon after I came here. Just about speak our lingo, though they was pretty wild, and carried spears and come straight from the desert. They come up to me and started pawing me around, so I dropped one and started in on the other. Then some more came, and there was a proper blue. After that things was OK and we was all cobbers.'

'And you went camping with them?'

'When I put it on the boss.'

'Oh, why put it on the boss?'

'Look, the boss is all right. So's his missus. He gives me a fair go and I give him one. He's my sponsor, see? So I don't stick him up. I ask if I can go camping with the blacks and he says why not. Do me good, get me used to the bush. Old MacBride

46

went and yelled to the policeman about it, and what d'you think? Harmon says if it's right with me boss it'll be right with him. Only time Harmon played ball with anyone in his life.'

Bony could detect the rebellion waning from the boy, and in its place, enthusiasm.

'Been away lots of times,' Tony went on. 'You know only for a couple of nights and not far away. Went huntin' with 'em, helped to fox a 'roo or two, and then took 'em back to the blacks' camp to eat. Good, too. Bit of a song and dance round the fire. Then a wrestle with some of 'em, and lying out lookin' up at the stars and sleeping' good till morning. And j'you know what, Nat? I got on good-ho with the lot of 'em. The boss said I would if I didn't muck about after the lubras ... didn't even look at 'em sideways. And that's how it is. Leave the skirts alone, and they're all good mates.

'I know how to dig for honey-ants, Nat,' continued Tony, momentarily released from inhibitions. 'Ever had a feed of ducks plastered with clay and buried in fire ashes so's they cook in their feathers? Look, them blacks can tell you anything. They see a track and say what bloke made it, and how long back he made it. And all them things.'

'They can be good friends, Tony. That was why the tracker said it wasn't you who went out to Lorelli's place and murdered his wife.'

'Yair, about it, Nat. Them blacks are good coves.'

CHAPTER 7

Digging for Nuggets

Foot-tracking is an art, and not, therefore, regarded by the courts as is the exact science of finger-printing. The wild aborigines have given examples of extraordinary proficiency, and for them foot-tracking is, indeed, an exact science.

Every morning Bony strolled along Main Street's sidewalks.

He observed countless imprints made by boots and even sand-shoes and bare feet. Following a person, and therefore establishing that that person made a particular set of foot-tracks, he memorized them and stored them in his mental card index, and if subsequently he came across the same tracks, he knew who made them.

He knew, too, when they were made, and so came to the knowledge that the town undertaker often visited a widow, who was a dressmaker, between the hours of nine and eleven in the evening. This, of course, was none of his business.

Patiently he sought for the tracks of the man who wore a size eight sandshoe when he committed two murders. That man could be wearing riding-boots, dancing-pumps, or sandals, and as he would walk the same, he would reveal the same peculiarities as when wearing sandshoes. His stride would be the same, the manner of his limp would be the same, and the way in which he placed his feet in juxtaposition with a central line would be the same.

At the end of a week Bony had not seen this man's tracks on Main Street, and now thought it probable that he lived at Dry-blowers Flat or at one of the cattle stations on the road to Laverton. He did refresh his memory by studying the imprints made by Constable Harmon's set of plaster casts, much to the satisfaction of the policeman. He found on the sidewalks foot-tracks much like them, and those of Tony Carr came very close.

He was completely confident that one day he would see the tracks he sought, and find the man who made them. Success is an edifice built on Patience.

He called on Sister Jenks one morning at the close of her surgery hour, and for excuse suggested a bottle of coloured water for a slight tummy ailment.

'H'm! Tummy pains, Bony. Well now, a nice draught of salts is an excellent remedy,' she said brightly, and he had to explain that the 'medicine' was intended as eyewash for the curious.

'So that's it, Bony. All you've come for is a gossip about the neighbours. Well, which one is it this time? Seriously, though, are you growing any warmer?'

'I could be sitting on an iceberg. Nothing pairs, nothing matches, nothing falls down and nothing builds up. There is a seemingly weak point I want to test. I keep returning, because there is nothing else to return to, to the poor reports on tracks which expert trackers could be expected to have made much more extensive. I've been thinking, as indeed have others, that our murderer chose to commit his killings when the tribe was away from Daybreak, hoping that the delay by having to bring in outside trackers would frustrate the police. There is a possible other reason he had for choosing his timing. Shall we discuss the MacBrides and their aborigine domestic?'

'Anything you like, Bony. You're anxious because there might be another murder, aren't you?'

'Were it not for that possibility, I could regard myself as being on holiday. Yes, I am anxious. Because I haven't forced action, I haven't yet met the MacBrides. Be my magnifying-glass. The parson . . . could he have had an affair with the dead girl?'

'Of course not, Bony. What an idea!'

'It has been known to happen,' murmured Bony, evincing slight embarrassment. 'I understand that the girl worked for the MacBrides for periods of weeks, and for similar periods lived with her people. Correct?'

'Yes.' Sister Jenks puckered her forehead in protest. 'But I don't think the MacBrides could be called her employers in the real sense. Mrs MacBride provided Mary with good clothes, and when she went anywhere in the car, she took Mary with her.'

'Well then, did Mary have any boy friends . . . black or white?'

'I don't think so. She had girl friends. I've seen her with some of the girls from Dryblowers Flat . . . white girls . . . the two Elder girls, as well as others.'

'The Elder girls, what are they morally, do you think?'

Sister Jenks laughed impishly.

'You know, Bony, I do believe you don't like asking about girls' morals, or even a parson's morals. Don't mind me. I've never heard anything against the morals of the Elder girls, and

49

I would have, had either given cause for gossip. They're as wild as brumbies. The other girls down there are, too. They go hunting with the aborigine girls, and I know that Mary used sometimes to be of the party.'

'Thank you, Sister. We have to remember that Mary at the time was living with the MacBrides. She went to bed about ten o'clock, and was then wearing the nightdress provided by Mrs MacBride. When she was found dead the next morning, she was wearing the old print frock provided by the Mission, and without which no aboriginal woman is permitted to come near Daybreak, or even Dryblowers Flat. Therefore, she must have put on that old print dress before leaving her room, and we can reasonably assume that she did so to go out into Main Street to meet her murderer.

'How did she compare with the other women of the tribe? Was she gay or serious? Was she personally clean? In short, was she attractive to men . . . white men especially?'

'I'll describe her for you,' offered Sister Jenks. 'Mary was, I'd say, about twenty. On regular food she became nicely rounded. She looked, what shall I say, she looked very nice in the clothes given her. She laughed a lot and spoke very little to anyone excepting Mrs MacBride, of whom I'm sure she was very fond.

'Now you've come to concentrate on Mary, you've made me, too, and I remember little things about her. I spoke to her after church on the Sunday morning before she was killed, and she seemed glum; not her usual happy self. I remember asking her if she was unwell. She shook her head. "I'm good-o, Miss," she said. She called every woman "miss" and every man "mister". Given another year with the MacBrides, I believe she would have spoken as well as most of us.'

'Forgive me for switching. What men in Daybreak have the name of being strongly interested in women in general, and so possibly in a woman like Mary?'

'You really think that sex is behind Mary's murder?'

'It's an angle which must not be ignored . . . How much or how little is your personal experience with the tribe, individuals, I mean?'

The cold crust of the hospital sister occupying a position of responsibility plus independent authority melted, to leave this girl warmly human. She burrowed among the débris of her desk and showed him a picture of some fifteen small naked babies lying in the sunshine, and seemingly guarded by two fierce half-bred dingoes.

'Aren't they sweet?' she said softly, waiting for his enthusiasm. 'Not one a day older than seven months and when the tribe comes back from walkabout I think there'll be five new ones.'

'You keep count of them?'

'Oh yes. And Constable Harmon helps, too. He thinks we've stopped that horrid infanticide in this local tribe. They're a long way from us, though. The young boys and girls are closer than the elders, and I suppose we ought to be grateful to white girls like the Elders and to one or two white lads like Tony Carr.'

'How d'you get along with Miss Harmon?'

'Very well. Nice old thing. Always letting the prisoners out, and that annoys her brother tremendously. Of course, they never attempt to go farther than the hotel, but the constable has to round them up and take them back. Then there's a frightful row. You heard about their tragedy, I suppose?'

Bony said he'd not heard, and Sister Jenks related that Harmon's wife and sister were riding in Esther Harmon's car back to Kalgoorlie one evening, when two youths in a stolen car crashed into them, killing Harmon's wife, and permanently crippling his sister.

'It's why he stays in Daybreak,' she went on. 'The boys, they were just under the twenty mark, weren't hurt, and ran away. Harmon happened to find them working on a station. The station men all had to join in to stop him killing them. There was quite an inquiry, and they sent Harmon out here, and now he won't agree to a transfer, and the heads aren't strong on forcing him to take a transfer. I think that's a lot to do with his treatment of Tony Carr. He seems to be just waiting for Tony to do something he shouldn't. He bullied Tony badly when Tommy Moss was found killed.'

'But why, d'you know?'

'Well, it seems that Tommy Moss never met Tony without calling him names, and one day Tony chased him into the garage and threatened that if he didn't stop it he'd put him in hospital. Two days later young Moss was found dead on the track beside his bike.'

'What is your opinion of Tony Carr?' asked Bony, and Sister Jenks came back swiftly:

'What's yours?'

'Same as your own,' he conceded laughingly, and shortly afterwards left to take over the bar service from Kat Loader.

The following day he rode down to Dryblowers Flat, finding it a town planner's nightmare, there being no hint of any planning. Ramshackle buildings of old iron, canegrass and hessian bags sprawled among the rather lovely sandalwoods on the banks of a dry creek in the bed of which a deep soak provided water of the purest quality.

The house inhabited by Elder and his daughters, though 'slapped' together, was at least commodius, clean and cool. Joy came to meet him, pat the horse's neck, and invite him in for a cup of tea. The injured foot was still bandaged, and today she was wearing a pair of her father's carpet slippers.

'It'll be all right in another week, Nat,' she informed him shyly, her golden eyes frankly admiring.

'I'm glad of that. I'll be able to tell a certain young man that he needn't bother to be worried about you any longer.'

'Tony Carr?'

Bony smiled. He was asked not to mention Tony's name to her father, and he winked brazenly. He was presented to Joy's sister, Janet, a rounded edition of herself, having the same-coloured hair, but eyes of penetrating grey. Elder was a 'young' man of seventy or so, and they found him in the shade of a rear shed, working on leather belts.

Elder thanked Bony for what he had done for Joy, and the girls went into the house to prepare afternoon tea. He had Janet's eyes, and they pin-pointed the visitor without a hint of rudeness. Himself of the Interior, he waited politely through several casual remarks to be told the visitor's business.

'I'd like to play poker, but haven't the time,' Bony said,

having made the inevitable cigarette. And Elder came back with: 'Banker's my game at the moment. Short shrift, win or lose.'

'All right, I lay my bet and play it fast. I'm riding Harmon's horse. I work at the pub. I am on a secret mission of inquiry into the death of Mary, for the Aborigines' Department. Sister Jenks told me you would respect a confidence, and not ask unwanted questions.'

'That lass is sound commonsensical, Nat.' The eyes of eternal youth gleamed with humour. 'Some debts a man can never pay; he can only try. You ask. I answer.'

'Thanks. We have reason to think that the aborigines haven't been a hundred per cent cooperative in helping to clear up that murder, and we're not satisfied it was a tribal killing. Been any trouble between them and anyone living in Daybreak, or outside?'

'Used to be a deal of it in the old days,' replied Elder. 'Got better after the present chief, called Iriti, took over. Melody Sam and the policeman who was here before Harmon arranged a sort of peace treaty. Since then they've acted right, and Melody's been generous to 'em with meat and tobacco every time they come in from walkabout.'

'Any trouble with the lubras and the whites?' pressed Bony, and Elder said there had been none since Harmon had got a man three years for having relations with a lubra. Then he mentioned Tony Carr, and Elder said:

'I got no time for that young feller, but he wouldn't be off hunting with the bucks for days on end if he was mucking about with black gals. Leastways, he wouldn't 've come back from a hunt.'

It was Elder's opinion that Mary's death was a ritual execution. She was becoming too attached to the parson and his wife, and when the excuse came to kill her, that was that, in Main Street or out in the desert. It didn't matter where, to them.

'What was the excuse?' Bony promptly wanted to know.

'Well, daughter Janet tells the story that she and Mary and other gals went camping out, and she and Mary came on an abos' ceremonial ground in the mulga forest down there. Happened about this time last year. None of us go into the forest, there being nothing in it to go for. The gals, you know, black and white, was away up on a rock hole to the north of the forest, and on the way back Janet said that, instead of coming round the outside of the forest, she'd go direct through it, and she kidded Mary to go with her.

'So through the forest they went, leaving the others to come back the long way round. As Janet tells it, they came to a mound of boulders, and from this mound they see the ceremonial ground all laid out in circles and things with white quartz. Mary got frightened and wouldn't go with Janet across the ground. She went round it and joined Janet on this side. She oughtn't to have been there. Taboo to a lubra. Good excuse to kill her for leaving the tribe for the whites, for that is what it looked like, even though she did spend a lot of time with her people. I can't understand why they didn't kill Janet, who did cross the ground.'

'Raise too much dust,' surmised Bony. 'And besides, a white girl would mean nothing in their scheme of things.'

CHAPTER 8

Melody Sam's Private Eye

No man was ever more grateful for service than was Melody Sam for being cured, cleaned and polished, and, like his stone counterpart, set up once more on his pedestal. The granddaughter continued to evince interest in quite an important question, viz. was the yardman married or single, and Constable Harmon's good fellowship, created by the taming of the grey horse, continued without ruffle.

Nine days had Inspector Bonaparte been at Daybreak, and he had listened and probed as he performed his duties and studied the currents beneath the surface of this normally placid community. He was no more conscious of the passing of time than the town goats, and was as indifferent to what his distant superiors might be thinking about his lack of reports as Bulow's Range was of the vast and silent mulga forest.

In mid-morning of the tenth day, he was seated with Melody Sam on the form outside the front of the hotel. There were no customers. Immediately before them was the pepper tree at that end of Main Street, with the stone man looking out to meet the road traveller from Laverton, or nearer station homesteads. Sam, who had not taken a drink for seven days, sat straight and strong, his feet encased in riding-boots, his legs imprisoned within gabardine trousers, his torso decorated by a white shirt, with a buttoned waistcoat of dark material, and a watch-chain of linked gold nuggets strung across his chest. His white hair was short and stiff. His moustache was short and bristling. His countenance, like that of his granddaughter, was polished like a gibber.

'Them pepper trees,' he remarked, 'I planted them back in '98. There was thirty of 'em, and we only lost one, and that one was chewed up by the ruddy goats. Had to guard 'em pretty close for the first ten years; after that they were too tough even for the goats. Another one we nearly lost, that third one down the row.' Melody Sam chuckled. 'He got nearly et by a feller we called. "Whispering Will". Someone bet him he wouldn't chew his way through a pepper tree, so he went out one night and gave it a go. Like the goats he found it a bit tough, so went home for the axe and chopped halfway through before we could snare the axe off him.'

'Sporting days,' drawled Bony.

'Before your time, Nat. Them days men got into it, boots and all, with rocks and axes and whatever come handy. Nowadays they sneak around and does folk in with a bludgeon or a knife across the windpipe, and for no reason anyone can make out.'

'I've been hearing about the Daybreak murders.'

'You would've, Nat. Got the police from Kal running round in circles, and poor old Harmon, well, he's all right in his way. We get along with him.'

'Must be a lunatic in Daybreak, or at Dryblowers.'

And again Melody Sam chortled.

'Plenty of wonkyites down at Dryblowers, but not that bad. Take a ride over that way and look-see for yourself. Characters, all of 'em. No, this feller murderin' people isn't that sort of lunatic. He's livin' hereabouts nice and peaceful, and one night he'll get his chance again. And then, Nat, I'm going to put you to work on him.'

'Oh, why me?'

'Because there's something crook about the trackers they got on the job. I'm not liking these murders. Pretty bad for our reputation. Daybreak's a good town. Exceptin' for a fight, or a wife-bashing, and a bit of thieving now and then, it could be said that Daybreak's a pure town. Has to be. She's my town. Excepting the post office and the police station and courthouse, I own her, lock, stock and barrel. Someone murders one of my folk, and he murders me. We got to catch him, Nat, and when we do I'm going to have Harmon tethered to one of them trees, and I'm goin' to sit in the courthouse in judgement, and fifteen minutes after I sentence our murderer, we'll have him hanging pop-eyed under one of them pepper trees.'

The vapouring of senility? No, the voice was hard, and the mind was clear and cold. Bony stirred uneasily, and, to conceal it, he began with tobacco and papers.

'Might cause a lot of strife,' he said.

'Bound to, Nat, bound to.'

That seemed that, with nothing to add. Bony said:

'What d'you think is crook about the trackers?'

'Well you keep this under your hat. You're workin' for Melody Sam, and no one's ever found him stingy. I like you, Nat, and we get along. 'Sides you never slavered when I was crook of the booze, or made me think I was wonky or something. I've watched you, You know more'n you say. Deep, Nat, and I like 'em deep when the deepness is straight. What are we paying you as yardman?'

'Ten pounds a week, and keep,' replied Bony, and wondered what he would do when given his wages. Worse was to come.

'A tenner a week,' growled Melody Sam. 'Used to be ten shillings a week, and they'd rush the job. A tenner a week, eh!

Well, I'm not paying you any more 'cos you wouldn't be worth it. That is as a yardman. Mind you, you're not doing too badly in the bar, but you got a lot to learn yet. It's this other job that's in me mind, this one about checking up on the trackers and getting right down to base when the next murder happens.'

'What was the matter with the trackers?' evaded Bony, now wondering how he was going to deal with the taxation fiends if his income were to rise by another ten, twenty or thirty pounds a week.

Melody Sam moodily watched the council staff sweeping pepper-tree débris into heaps, and slowly nearing the hotel. It seemed that he had to marshal his facts.

'There's that abo girl, Nat,' proceeded Melody Sam. 'She wasn't a bad looker. Not above twenty or twenty-one. You know what some of 'em are like at that age.' An iron-hard elbow dug into Bony's ribs, and a soft chuckle hinted that Melody Sam knew what they were like at that age. 'She was knocked on the head right under the far pepper tree, and opposite the Manse. She was working for the parson at the time, had been, off and on, for a year. They reckoned they'd made a Christian out of her, but ... Now it so happened that Harmon had a tracker called Abie, and this Abie cleared away with the tribe before the parson's maid was murdered, so that Harmon didn't have a tracker on hand.

'It seems that Abie feller was after the lubra, and Harmon got the idea he could have come in from the desert and killed her. Anyway, he had brain enough to have all the ground, about where the girl was found, covered with sheets and things to preserve the tracks, and he telephoned the policeman down at Laverton to bring his tracker along to help prove his point. The Laverton black was brought, four days later, and he said an aborigine had killed the girl, and then he thought it was a white man. He wasn't sure, and no amount of bullying him could make him sure. In fact, the place there at the far end of Main Street was naturally churned up by people and goats and a cow or two.

'And the police went no further, or didn't seem to. Harmon

made up his mind it was Abie who did it, and he sat tight and waited for the blacks to come in again, and Abie with 'em. When they did, Abie wasn't among 'em, and no one's seen him since.

'Lot of people thought at the time it was a tribal murder. You know, the wench being promised to one buck and another buck stepping in and scooping the pool. Harmon thought that, but the parson wouldn't have it. He's all for the blacks and agin' the whites. Did quite a bit of crowing when the second murder happened. You heard about that?'

'Yes, a Mrs Lorelli,' replied Bony. 'Young Carr was telling me he was suspected of it.'

'Easier to suspect me,' snorted Melody Sam. 'All that young bastard wants is a couple of floggings and a spell of training. I had to exert meself about him. This time again the blacks are away in the back of beyond, and Harmon got two up from Kalgoorlie. They picked up the tracks of a bloke wearing sand-shoes; he'd come from the bed of a stony creek, done his killing with his hands.'

'It was then decided that Tony Carr was a likely suspect?' Bony interjected.

'Yes.' Melody Sam raised his great voice. 'Hey, you, Bert Ellis! It's only just gone eleven, and you don't get to no drink till your dinner hour starts.' The council staff protested and was told to keep to hell out of it until noon. Melody Sam snorted, controlled his voice, went on: 'The working man! Look at him! Twelve quid a week, and I could do more in four hours than he does in eight . . . Yes, they tried to hang it on young Carr. He admitted he was at the homestead about sundown, and when the husband got home at nine o'clock his wife had had her life squeezed out. When I say "they", I mean Harmon, egged on by the parson. MacBride's been here a bit too long. Thinks he owns the place. He don't even own the church. I do. I pay his screw. I says they don't arrest young Carr, not with the evidence of them sandshoes.'

Melody Sam chuckled his dry, soft chuckle, saying:

'When I opens me mouth, Nat, they all droop. Anyway, nothing come out of that Mrs Lorelli murder. They brought the plain-clothes men from Kalgoorlie, and they hunted around for a couple of weeks, and spent most of their wages in my pub. Good for business. Same thing happened when the lad, Moss, got his throat slit out near the mine, only they stayed longer and spent more on beer. Same sandshoes, Nat. Same man wearing them. And – this is where you'll come in, Nat – the same lies told about them sandshoe tracks by the blacks.'

'Just a minute,' interposed Bony. 'Did that lubra, Mary, always stay . . .?'

'You hold your horses, Nat,' growled Melody Sam. 'I'm tellin' this yarn. We'll get back to her some time. It's them sandshoe tracks now, and I'm the boss, remember.'

'Sorry,' humbly murmured Inspector Bonaparte.

'Good! Now when the abo wench was killed and the Laverton tracker pointed out the tracks, Harmon didn't have the sense to send for plaster of paris and make casts of 'em. But he did make casts of the sandshoe tracks at the Lorelli homestead, and at the mine, about the young Miss killing. He's got two sets of print casts, and he's got two reports on 'em. Follow me?'

'Yes . . . I think so,' replied Nat the yardman.

'You will in a minute. Now, there's three murders; there's two plaster casts of the same set of sandshoe tracks; and there are three reports got off the blacks in different parts of the country. The sandshoe tracks agree, and the reports agree. Understand?'

'Yes,' replied Bony.

'Now, take the trackers' reports as one. It says the feller wearing the sandshoes had a size eight foot, is a white feller, and would weigh round about 160 pounds (their estimate being on the weight of Constable Harmon), and that he limps with the right leg. And that's all. Now wait.'

Melody Sam rose and stepped off the hard sidewalk to the dusty road of Main Street. He strode over to his statue, where he turned to face outward along the road to Laverton, and returned to the seat.

'No mucking things up, Nat,' he said. 'You go see my tracks and tell what you read in 'em.'

Bony obliged.

'They are the tracks of a white man, wearing size eight boot. He weighs about 140 pounds. He's an old man but still strong walkabout feller. He has been sick, but has recovered from the sickness. He placed the toe of his left foot farther out than usually, intending to deceive me, his tracker.'

'Ah!' breathed Melody Sam. 'I thought so. I been thinking so. Now you tell me this, Nat, you tell me why them black trackers didn't read more into them sandshoe tracks than they let out. Why, I had an abo lad once who could have told me more about that murderer than the feller ever knew about himself, and those three trackers were all the same ... ruddy experts. All they say is that he's white, that he has a size eight, that he weighs as much as Harmon or me, and that he limps a bit. Nothing else. Why, that boy I had could have told me what the feller et for dinner, or got close to it.'

'H'm!' emitted Bony, secretly admiring this knowledgeable old quartz reef. 'I see what you've got on your mind.'

'Good! Then you see what I want you here for. I want you right on the job when the next killing is done, and then you can tell as much about the killer as those three black bastards must know, and kept to themselves.'

'Think the police could have kept it back to help in their investigation?' asked Bony.

'Sure they didn't,' promptly countered Melody Sam.

'Seems like we'll have to wait for another killing,' Bony said calmly, to match the mood of his seat companion.

'Yes, seems we shall, Nat. Nothing makes sense. As Harmon says, there's no plan, no sensible tie-up with even two murders, let alone the three. One black, two white. Two women, one man, the lad. One woodened with a waddy or something, one with his throat cut, one strangled. Harmon's got a book over there called *A Thousand Homicides*. We been reading it up. There's nothing in it like our Daybreak murders. You want a drink?'

'No. What about you?'

'When I'm off it, I'm off it, Nat. Cripes! Where did he jump from?'

On the Laverton road stood a naked black figure gazing

60

towards them. His hair was bunched high above his forehead. He stood straight, and was less than medium height.

'Hey you, come here!' shouted Melody Sam. The aborigine advanced. 'Well, I'm blowed, Nat. This here is Harmon's tracker, Abie.'

CHAPTER 9

The Barman's Morning

He was still young. Three short cicatrices across his midriff had but recently healed. As with all these western inland tribes, his legs were mere spindles, his hips were narrow, his chest was deep, and his shoulders slightly sloping. The stomach was shrunken and hard, and the hands, the one holding a short stick and the other two six-foot spears, were big, compared with the size of the thin, sinewy arms.

Standing at the edge of the sidewalk, his splayed feet shuffled the dust, and being confronted by the eyes of white men, his own were restless, and never met their gaze.

'You been long time, Abie,' began Melody Sam. 'You been bring letter-stick, eh? Give it.'

The short stick was offered. It was about six inches in length, and had been scraped by a quartz or granite chip, scorched by fire and polished by sandstone mixed with saliva. Two encircling cuts gave the stick three divisions, and within two of the divisions, short cuts had been made, the third division untouched. It was, as Bony knew, as indeed did old Melody Sam, a ceremonial letter-stick.

Melody Sam put forth his hand, and the stick was placed on it. The old man studied the markings, nodded sagely, looked up into the steady eyes watching him. Now, Bony knew that Sam, the white man, had been initiated into this desert tribe. He put out his hand for the letter-stick, and downward flashed the spears barring his hand from it.

Who was he to touch that letter-stick which had been adequately 'sung' with magic brought from afar and rubbed into churinga stones, and from the churinga stones rubbed into the message of goodwill? As he stood, the points of the spears rose with him, now two feet of driving space between them and his chest. The points were of fire-toughened mulga. Without haste, Bony pulled his shirt up from the belted trousers, and revealed the cicatrices marking his body.

The dark eyes in the chocolate-skin face glistened, the spear points were lowered and then swept upward as the hafts were pressed against a hard shoulder. Bony thrust the shirt hem into place and sat down. Again he offered to take the stick, and this time was permitted. Melody Sam waited, then chuckled saying:

'Got you bluffed, Nat.'

'This is a special stick, Sam,' Bony replied. 'This stick is from the chief to another chief – you Sam. It says two nights and one day. After that, as you remarked, it has me bluffed. Excepting, of course, that you have been properly sealed into their tribe.'

Melody Sam beamed his pleasure.

'Good on you, Nat! That's the boy. You're better than I thought. Yes, the stick says the mob will be coming in early the day after tomorrow, and will I have plenty big tucker for 'em.'

He spat on the dust at his feet, stooped and pressed into the spittle the end of the stick which had no markings. Then, lightly touching his forehead with this same end, he presented it to the 'postman' for return delivery. Abie accepted the stick in his left hand, and there it would remain until delivered. He smiled, looked from one to the other, that the smile should include both, and was about to turn away when Melody Sam said:

'Wait! You been see Constable Harmon?'

The aborigine shook his head. Sam offered a two-ounce plug of chewing tobacco, and Abie gracefully accepted it. Sam said:

'Then you been clear out fast. Constable Harmon catch you,

he been kickum your backside, you been no more his tracker.'

Abie revealed at last his racial sense of humour. He pursed his lips and made the sound known to the white civilization as 'the raspberry', laughed, turned about, strode away to the Laverton road, and seemed to vanish in his own foot dust.

'You know, Nat,' said Melody Sam, 'they call 'em "nigs", they call 'em savages, they call 'em this and that, but they're the only decent people living in the world today. And d'you know what? The sloppy fools down in the cities want to have 'em brought in and made to live in houses and go to work, and eat pork and beef off china plates, and all that. I don't hold with it. I don't hold with forcing them people into our own dirty, murderous, sinful state we call civilization.'

'I'm with you there, Sam,' agreed Bony. 'What was the full message?'

'Oh, they'll be coming to Daybreak some time the day after tomorrow. Been away many weeks, living on goannas and things, and putting their young men through the initiation hoops, and the young gals turned into women. See Abie's stomach? Flat as a board. So Iriti, the old man, sends me word, knowing that there'll be a beast ready slaughtered for 'em to guzzle and cram their stomachs and make 'em sleep for a week.'

'You always kill the fatted calf?' inquired Bony warmly.

'Why not?' replied Sam. 'We run our cattle over their land. We get taxed for it, but the abos don't get the taxes. So I give a beast when they come in from their walkabouts.'

'Good to see that Abie didn't keep away from Daybreak because he was frightened of being accused of killing the parson's maid,' Bony said. 'Those welts on his mid-section weren't done ten years ago.'

'No!'

'No. He's been away all this time on tribal business.'

'Musta been. Likely enough the tribal business of being cut about to get on with his initiation. I had the idea it was all done at the same time.'

'Not always, and not everywhere. That aborigine girl, Mary, did she always remain when the tribe went on walkabout?'

63

'It was the first time she did stay back, and the last, but that wouldn't bring her relations into it, would it, Nat?'

'No, by no means.'

'What I thought,' agreed Sam. 'That gal was murdered by this sandshoe-wearing white bastard, all right. And one of these days them abos is goin' to sniff him out, and we'll have another killing. I won't have . . .'

'Hey Sam, it's gone twelve o'clock,' wailed a voice, and over by the end pepper tree, giving shadow to the stone Melody Sam, stood the council staff. Sam whipped his enormous time-keeper from its waistcoat pocket, glanced at it, lurched to his feet and glared at Bony.

'Fine sort of yardman you are, Nat,' he shouted. 'Gone noon, and no one to serve the population with a drink. Get to your bar, man.' Abruptly lowering his voice he went on: 'I'm goin' to yabber with Harmon about them abos coming in. And don't you forget you are hired twice, and twice the wages of ten pounds a week and keep.'

Detective-Inspector Napoleon Bonaparte nodded gravely, rose and entered the bar with the council staff treading on his heels.

'Hard doer, ain't he?' grumbled the council staff, smoothing the wispy grey moustache, and leaning with Australian elegance against the bar counter.

'You mean the boss,' surmised Bony, pulling beer. 'I don't believe he's over eighty.'

'He is, though. Luck! I been here in Daybreak thirty-eight years, and when I came he was just the same as he is now. He don't alter.'

'He was telling me he owns the town, even the church.'

'He owns everything, Nat,' responded Ellis solemnly. 'All of Daybreak and a couple million acres round about Daybreak. Was that Abie you and him was talkin' to?'

'Melody Sam said he was.'

'What's to do? Did he say?'

'That the mob will be coming in the day after tomorrow. Old Sam promised them a beast.'

'Always gives 'em plenty of tucker when they come in,' Ellis

64

said, approvingly. 'Nobody ever yet starved in Daybreak. He'll be telling Fred Joyce to kill a extra beast tomorrow night.'

'You said Sam owns a lot of land. Runs cattle on it?'

'Not himself he don't. Has partners to run them places. He don't do much himself outside the pub, and there's times when the pub wouldn't pay for itself. Not like it usta be. Not the people round about now. Not the gold to be found. Thirty years ago there was three hundred prospectors living at Dryblowers; now there's not more than fifteen. Trade'll buck up later today, though. Always does mail day. Fill 'er up, Nat, then I'll be gettin' home for lunch.'

'Where will the blacks be camping?' asked Bony, topping up the glass following the subsidence of the collar.

'Generally at the north end of Bulow's Range. Down a bit there's a lot of surface granite, and they got rock holes there. Then there's another camp over the mulga. Have their ceremonies in there, and plants their chief men there, too. I never been in that forest. People say it's the best mulga forest in the State. I don't care if it is. Daybreak's forest is enough for me.'

Several men entered the bar, and the council staff left. All wanted to know if the strange aborigine was Harmon's one-time tracker, and it was apparent that the entire township was aware of the visit. Bony could not but observe the demeanour of these townsfolk, for their nonchalance was unusual in view of crimes of violence of comparatively recent date. Everyone seemed normally alert, and it could not be said they were bucolic. He could detect no undercurrents of fear or suspicion or mass emotion.

Fred Joyce, the butcher and Tony's employer, came in for a drink, smiled at the barman, and, when opportunity occurred, asked Bony if he would break in a couple of colts.

'Harmon's pretty pleased with his grey, Nat,' he said. 'Told me he's got wonderful action and enough stamina to win the Melbourne Cup.'

'That's a grand horse, Fred,' Bony responded. 'He came to it easy, and if Harmon toughens him gradually he'll have a sure winner.'

'Well, you think about them two I want broken in, will you? Only hack on the job is the old dead-beat young Tony rides, and he'll never ride properly if he don't get on something a bit more lively. Besides, as it is, he takes too much time rounding up the cattle.'

Bony drifted to serve others, and presently came back to attend to Joyce.

'Think you'll make much of that feller? Carr, I mean. Seems a bit sullen.'

'Lot of good in him; lot of bad, Nat. No chance. Dragged up by the back hair. Father a drunk, mother worse. Jailbirds both of 'em. Wonder is how kids like him ever lived beyond day-old babies. Tony's in the Victoria Delinquent School before he's ten. And he's in and out as fast. You know, escaping, pinching cars, selling parts. Up the grade to bashings, and knocking women about for their handbags. And then the great break. Hitch-hiked, jumped the rattlers all the way across the Null-arbor to Kalgoorlie. There he sticks me up, and after a lot of trouble I went bail for him and got him out. And halfway on the track to Daybreak he tried to nab my car.'

Bony worked, and returned to the butcher.

'Tony tried to take the car from you,' he prompted.

'Nearly tricked me, too,' Joyce said grimly. 'I give him the biggest belting of his life. Game as they come, he was, but when I'd conquered him he'd both eyes bunged up, four teeth knocked out, a broken rib Sister Jenks had to set when I got him here. And, Nat, ever since as quiet as a lamb.'

'You think he'll settle down?'

'Doubt it sometimes,' replied Joyce. 'What's bred, you know. Men are like horses: good, indifferent, bad. And some just plain hopeless. If Tony don't settle down here he never will anywhere else. Trouble is, the kid's record's against him. No one here'll give him a fair go exceptin' my wife, and, you wouldn't believe it, Miss Harmon, the policeman's sister.'

'Speaks well enough of you,' Bony said, and Joyce laid his huge hands on the counter, and clenched his fists.

'Tony never forgot these,' he said. 'We never had any kids. If I'd had sons I would never have had to use these on 'em. Why?

66

They would have been slapped early in the piece, like I was, and you, I suppose, and like most law-abiding men. Kids are like colts. Well, be seeing you. Think about them colts I want breakin'.'

Joyce departed, and presently the others left in a bunch. Bony was polishing glasses when Melody Sam appeared with Constable Harmon. There being no customers, Constable Harmon breasted the counter. He named his drink, Sam called for ginger ale, and both were served by Inspector Bonaparte.

'You taking the grey out this afternoon, Nat?' Harmon suggested. 'Still has some rough edges, as you'll agree.'

Like Joyce the butcher, Harmon was large, and he also had hands like grappling-irons. His small hazel eyes were friendly and his voice was warm. Horse made him human, and horse was the link between himself and any other man who also was horse.

'Yes, if the boss won't mind,' Bony agreed, and Melody Sam snorted, and said the barman could have every afternoon off.

Melody Sam had passed to the cupboard in the rear wall and from it took his violin, wrapped lovingly in cloth. He proceeded to wax the bow and deftly tune the strings.

'Was wonderin' when the old boy would get around to his music,' whispered Harmon. 'Fill her up, Nat, and I'll get going. Don't forget to tell him he plays good, and he's your uncle for life.'

Melody Sam began to play, and the policeman drained his glass, winked at Bony and departed. Bony fell to polishing the used glasses and Melody Sam passed to the front entrance and stepped outside, still playing. When Bony went to the door, he saw Sam wandering down Main Street under the pepper trees, and being greeted by dogs that sat back and howled.

CHAPTER 10

Sounds Within the Silence

That the northern end of Bulow's Range was the highest point was proved by the surveyor's trig built there with boulders to form a tall cairn, and on the afternoon the aborigines were due to return from walkabout Bonaparte sat on the summit of the cairn, and his horse stood drowsily aside. The great arc of the horizon extending from the western edge of the mulga forest, round to the tips of several residuals rising above it, and so on round to the eastern limitless lands, confronted Bonaparte with that part of his ego from which there was no escape, and which, like love itself, there is never real desire to escape.

Sunlight creates shadows. The cairn's shadow stretched shortly to the east, topped with the shadow of this man. Vast cloud-shadows quilted the ground canopy of sparse scrub and browned glass plains. There were shadows about the great rocks at the feet of Bulow's Range, where also were the aborigines' hidden stores of water. Shades rather than shadows; soft light rather than shades. For in all this world there were no dark places, no black set against white, while the ruling tints of browns and greens were subject to the masses of amber and white diamonds tossed away by the great Being who first had possessed this land with eagerness to explore all its beauties.

Had Bonaparte slewed on his rocky set, he would have seen just below the summit of the Range the red track leading upward from Dryblowers Flat to merge into the northern end of Daybreak. And he would have been confronted with that other part of his ego which, also like love itself, demanded so much of him, and from which too he had no desire to escape. No man can serve two masters; but two masters may own a slave.

Of recent hours servitude to the one had been exacting, and

his soul needed the balance of the other. Throughout the previous two nights he had flitted about Daybreak, watching, waiting for, and hoping to frustrate a further strike by the Daybreak murderer, before the return of the aborigines. Again the duality of his ego tortured him. The hunter instinct was an ogre smacking its lips at the prospect of fresh blood to bring a new scent of a quarry to run down; the civilized part of him dreaded a violence which could spring only from the hellish depth of a human mind.

But the killing lust had lain quiescent throughout these two nights, for to what else could those three seemingly senseless murders be attributed? There was no pattern provided by the victims of this Daybreak murderer. The victims of such a one may be street walkers, or young girls attending colleges, or boys who have never shaved; or even elderly women and elderly men. They fall into a pattern from which the type of killer can be built into reasonable clarity.

A young aboriginal woman, a middle-aged housewife, and an apprentice lad of white parents! How could such provide a pattern? The first killed with a blunt instrument; the second strangled; the third killed with a knife across the throat. There was no pattern in method. There was a pattern in the timing, which was not of the night, but of the absence of the local aboriginal tribe which could have provided tracking experts with a minimum loss of time. This pattern did indicate a killer of deep cunning, a killer who was over the borderline of sanity but far from complete mental derangement. He wore special footwear, indicative of forethought, of planning ability.

It was this ability, allied with the unusual paucity of detail in the reports of the trackers, which created a stridently unusual problem for this man of two races who sat on a high stone and moodily peered over a world which had been withered by centuries of aridity, and yet had not died, and would never die.

The weakness in the armour of the problem was in this local aboriginal tribe. It was a problem having roots delving deep into a land claimed by Melody Sam. It was a problem not to be attacked hopefully by the scientific minds of any police organization. It could be likened to a giant boulder down there on the hillside, one of those boulders no man could upset to send crashing to the bottom, but which a colony of tiny ants could unseat, with their ceaseless burrowings.

And there, beyond the boulders guarding the secret sources of life, came those who owned this land with a spiritual passion beyond the understanding of the white man who had dispossessed them. Bony could see them, a long straggling line lengthening across an open space so filled with the diamond specks of mica, and so distant, that it was like a growing crack extending across a golden salver.

They were not coming home, those hundreds of beings. They had no home; they had never known the meaning of home nor needed to know its meaning. They owned nothing; everything – every tree and boulder, hill and creek-bed; every grain of sand and every mica speck – owned them. Only the dead possessed homes. They found their homes in tree-trunks, in boulders, in hillocks, in stony glades. They, the living, were journeying on, ever journeying from place to place within the borders of their tribal land, and pausing awhile to tidy here a ceremonial ground, and there a grave mound, and here beside a water hole to rest and take courage from the visiting birds and rodents to whose totems they belonged. In the secret places the young men had been initiated, and sealed into the tribe, and the young girls had been initiated into the duties of womanhood, and proudly these young members walked, and proudly bore the still smarting brands of initiation.

Eventually the leaders of the human chain emerged from the low and spare scrub on to the open ground extending all about Bulow's Range, and now Bony could see the individuals. The leaders and the initiated men carried spears, the hafts of which had been traded with far southern aborigines who live in the great forests where saplings grew straight and long. The men walked in groups; the women and the children came straggling in the rear, the women loaded like camels with firewood, others with infants slung to hips; the older children running and jumping, and in obvious anticipation of distended bellies.

For over in the butcher's yard young Tony Carr had just shot a beast and was honing his knives to skin and make ready to hand it over to the travellers.

The leaders came up the slope, their eyes directed to the great boulders in which still lived the spirits of their ancestors, and higher still to note the man seated on the white-feller heap of stones, which Melody Sam had told them in the long ago they must not touch. At a distance from the boulders all but the leaders halted to gather into a waiting crowd. The leaders, four of them, came on up the slope and then parted to enter the maze of boulders, to see what had happened among them, if anything, during their absence.

Satisfied that all was well, they mounted the slope towards the waiting Bonaparte, having refrained from drinking at the rock holes of cold water, and keeping their people waiting also, until etiquette had been observed. Bonaparte, aware that they would know all about him from Abie's report, visually examined them. One was white of hair, thin, like his spears, of which he carried three, and possessed of a white beard looking as though one of the town goats had nibbled at it. He would be Chief Iriti. There was the medicine doctor, a tubby man of middle age, his black hair bunched high by a ribbon of human hair encircling his forehead. There was a very tall, lanky man of deceptive physical powers, and the late initiate, Abie the police tracker. Save for the pubic tassel and the small dilly-bag suspended from the neck by human hair string, they were entirely naked.

Arrived to within a hundred feet, they paused to set their spears on the ground, advanced a further twenty feet, and squatted, stilled like four ebony Buddhas resting on grey slate. They had thus obeyed the rules of approaching a stranger's camp without arms, indicating peaceful intent, and, by squatting politely, waited for invitation to enter the stranger's camp.

Etiquette! Practised for thousands of years. And behind it all the iron of tradition and the inelastic thongs of discipline. They had come to talk with the stranger, he who was one of them more than he could be one of the white-fellers. Should he be flash-feller, should he be white-feller-boss, they would talk to him and he would talk to them just the same, but without observance of etiquette.

The hotel yardman-cum-barman, not the detective-inspector, slid himself down the trig to the ground, where he removed his shirt and undervest. From the saddle bag he took four two-ounce plugs of tobacco, which he placed on the ground and dropped his hat over them. Then, standing erect, he raised one arm in time honoured invitation.

The visitors rose and slowly came forward. Of grave aspect, their dark eyes missed nothing, as their gaze moved over and about this stranger. Abie and the tall one remained a little behind the chief and the medicine man, and these slowly moved round Bony to inspect the cicatrices on his body. They hurrumphed without indicating satisfaction or otherwise, and then stood with the other two, and waited for the host to act. The host, with the toe of a boot, kicked the hat off the tobacco plugs, and gravely nodded to them to accept the gift. By common consent, host and visitors squatted on their heels.

Each of the four faces opposed to Bony bore the expression of a judge waiting to hear evidence. On them was neither hostility nor welcome, neither chill nor warmth. This was the stranger's camp, but the stranger was in their country. His initiation, plus the mark of the chief medicine-man of a far-away people, they had read in the cicatrices on his chest and back, and now they waited to learn his business in this their country, so distant from his own.

Bony was prepared, having co-opted Melody Sam. He told them he had been passing through their country on his own affairs, when, arriving at Daybreak, the white-feller policeman wanted a horse broken to saddle, and that Melody Sam had wanted him to investigate the murders, as the white-feller policeman had fallen down on his chest. It was the truth, and plain for them to understand, but they were less amenable when he blamed them for having been away when the murders had been committed, and went on to scorn Abie's tracking powers, and to mock the efforts of the trackers brought from distant places. Thus he became the judge, and they the defendants, without loss of poise and without hurt to their natural dignity.

'You fellers know Melody Sam,' Bony went on with calm equal to their own. 'Ole Melody Sam good white-feller. Time you come to Daybreak, he give you one big bullock feller, and then he give you plenty tobacco and plenty flour. You all sit-um down and eat and eat, and smoke and smoke. Ole Melody Sam good feller, he do this for you-all. Then killum-feller he come like Kurdatia and basham your lubra, and killum white woman and young white-feller. Old Melody Sam don't like this killing. This killing plenty bad for Melody Sam and all white-feller living in Daybreak. Daybreak belonga Melody Sam. You have killings in your country, you no like that, eh? Too right, Melody Sam don't like killings in his country.'

No change of facial expression. But shutters lowered before the eyes, which remained open and hard and blank, shutters which shut themselves in the recesses of their minds, and barred him out.

Bony told them that Melody Sam had given him a job in his hotel, and had asked him to investigate these Daybreak crimes, crimes which included the killing of one of their own women. Carefully avoiding insult, he lashed them for their indifference towards this particular murder, and claimed that among his own people no killer would have remained hidden and unpunished.

Their reaction? One of blank, stone-like imperviousness. The white man would have been infuriated: Bonaparte accepted the inferences stemming from their attitude of mind. They had shut him out, not because he was a stranger, but because he was old Melody Sam's private eye. Standing, he pointed away to the crow-dots whirling about the killing-yards, and they stood with him, and now the shutters were up, and their faces were lit with half-smiles, like the faces of children forgiven for some misdemeanour.

'Tony Carr he bin killum bullock,' Bony said, almost gaily. 'You eat and eat and eat, all right.'

'Too right!' exploded young Abie, and the medicine-man grunted and grinned. 'Too right!' haltingly repeated the chief, and eased his empty stomach by pressing his bony hands into the valleys of it.

Mounting his horse, Bony waved to them to accompany him and they shouted to their fellows below. Whereupon the lubras set wood in a pile, and fired it with a live firestick which they had brought all the way from the previous night's camp fire, and the men and the children came racing up the hill to join the elders.

Riding in their midst, Inspector Bonaparte might have been a general entering Rome; when he was but a half-caste taking a mob of 'savages' to a feast.

CHAPTER II

George Who Wasn't George

Generations of men have sat on the topmost rail of stockyards watching a horsebreaker at work, or just sitting and nattering in the presence of a yard full of horses or cattle. There is nothing more uncomfortable to sit on than a rail, but then what is comfort when the points of a horse or a steer are to be summed up and discussed?

There was a horse yard in a corner of the police station compound, and this morning there sat on the topmost rail Constable Harmon, Melody Sam, Fred Joyce and Bony. In the yard stood the constable's splendid grey gelding, and Bony's two horses, that by comparison were merely runts to look at, but tough as wiregrass to work. The animals were lazily swishing flies with their tails, and the men were as lazily doing nothing. It was enough that men and horses were closely together.

'Did you have to give those black bastards a whole bullock?' Harmon asked Melody Sam. 'They'll all be that gutted with beef that Abie won't be fit to work again for a week. I don't like being without a tracker.'

'Things are quiet enough,' mildly observed the butcher. 'No new murders or anything.'

'Just so, Fred,' agreed the policeman. 'No new murders or anything ... yet.'

'You think we can expect another?'

'Any time, Fred. Once a killer starts he can't let up.'

'True enough,' Melody Sam contributed. 'But with the murders we had, the blacks were on walkabout. They won't be going on walkabout again for a week or two. Why worry? We got Nat here if Abie don't show up, and I'm not climbing a tree to take me hat off to Abie ... or any other of the tribe.'

Harmon was morosely chewing a stem of barley grass, his big body relaxed so that he was like a bag of chaff balanced on a wire. Joyce sat with his hat tilted to the back of his head, and his frank grey eyes were puckered against the sunlight.

'I reckon Nat here'll tell us more about them sandshoe tracks than the abos,' Melody Sam continued. 'That is, if we have another murder.'

'We'll have another one,' growled Harmon. 'Bound to. And I'll be ready for it. I'm going to be right on Tony's wheel when it happens.'

'Aw, give the kid a go,' argued Joyce. 'He might've been a no-hoper, but he ain't done anything bad since he's been here.'

The silence which fell among them indicated their hope that the policeman would carry on, and when it was evident that Harmon would not, Bony said:

'Could be there won't be another murder. What makes you think there will be?'

'That book the constable's got called *A Thousand and One Murders*,' replied Melody Sam. 'It's all in there. Serial numbers they call these repeats done by one man. He gets a lift out of his killings. Does 'em all the same way.'

'But our killer don't do 'em all the same way,' objected Joyce, and the policeman countered with:

'He doesn't have to do 'em the same way. He gets his kick through feeling 'em perish from a weapon, like a blunt instrument or a carving-knife. I know how they start. They start being at war with the world, and go through street fights, then robberies, fouling milk-bars, and so on till one night they get in a

75

fight and smell blood, and that's when they become tigers. That's why the only likely bastard we got here in Daybreak is young Tony Carr. There's no one else that fits.'

'Well, I still think you're wrong,' Joyce said, and twisted about, preparatory to lowering himself to the ground. 'See you after. I got work to do.'

'And I'd better get back to me labours, too,' remarked Melody Sam. 'You can stay put if you want to, Nat, havin' done your chores and no customers about this morning.'

Slyly he winked at Bony, turned about, and strode from the compound, his back straight, shoulders squared, ready to pound the teeth in of any liar who claimed to have seen him a woeful victim of booze. It is the periodic drinker, not the habitual, who lives to be a hundred. The policeman said:

'That grey's still a bit of an outlaw, Nat. I'd shoot him if it wasn't for his smooth action. Feller has to have his mind on him all the time.'

'Sorry you're not satisfied, Mr Harmon.'

'Oh, that's all right, Nat. I'm satisfied well enough. You've done wonders with the bastard. As you know, some colts never turn out any good. They're like some humans. Kindness, firmness, anything you like, is sheer waste of time. What d'you reckon? You keep on with him?'

'Yes, if you wish,' assented Bonaparte, well aware that some men, no matter how good on a horse, are invariably bad with a horse. Men like Harmon have not that spiritual affinity with a horse which achieves perfect accord and coordination between man and beast. Someone was cooee-ing, and Harmon stirred and began reversing the pose preparatory to going to ground. 'That'll be morning tea. Better come over and have some.'

When both were off the fence, he said:

'You know, Nat, you're a strange feller. Don't talk much, think a lot. Should have been in the Force. You'd have done better than me at that.'

Morose, hard, bitter, Harmon was a man whose brain had been scarred by the blows of life, and recalling what Sister Jenks had said of Harmon's personal tragedy, Bony assumed cheerfulness.

'I'll keep with the grey, Mr Harmon. Never beaten by a horse yet. As for being a policeman, I'd be no good. Tried once over in Brisbane, and the instructor at the barracks said I'd never be a policeman's bootlace.'

Harmon led the way into the kitchen of his quarters, where his sister had tea and cake set out for them. She smiled at Bony with her dark eyes, but her voice was a trifle sharp when she bade him be seated at the table. When she brought the teapot from a corner of the stove, her left leg swung wide in that pathetic motion which people tried not to notice and never really succeeded.

'Horses!' she exclaimed. 'Give a man a horse, and nothing else interests him. Like a very small boy with a pup. How are you liking being at Daybreak, Nat?'

'Well enough, Miss Harmon,' replied Bony. 'People are friendly. Job is good, and Melody Sam isn't a hard boss.'

Harmon chuckled with very little mirth when he said:

'You got round him, Nat, like a good 'un. Next you'll be getting round Kat. I noticed the gleam in her eye yesterday.'

'Well, I never!' breathed his sister, lowering herself into a chair.

'No good to me,' Bony countered, with conviction. 'I'm not settling down in Daybreak, or anywhere.'

'So you say,' growled Harmon. 'Those Loader women always get what they go for. Fred Joyce reckoned he wasn't going to settle down. Wasn't going to give up the bright life for no woman on earth. A wild colonial boy, no woman was going to tame him. So he said a million times.'

'And you're meaning to tell us that Kat Loader's casting eyes at Nat, here?' pressed the interested Esther Harmon.

'I'm not meaning to tell anything,' growled her brother. 'You women always will take a man too serious. Pity you don't take me serious in the right places. I'll be locking up young Jacks over lunch, and if you go letting him out you'll be for it.'

'And what's he been doing?' asked Esther Harmon sharply.

'Milking Mrs Eccers's goats on the sly. She caught him at it late yesterday. Second time. First time his father gave him a hiding; this time his father asked me to deal with him before Mrs Eccers lays a complaint. As though I haven't any office work to do, nothing at all but help parents train their children.' He lurched to his feet. 'See you after, Nat.'

Grimly Esther Harmon waited until her brother left for his office.

'He's all right under it all, Nat. You'll let me call you Nat? I suppose you've heard what happened to us down in Kal?'

'Yes, Miss Harmon. That was too bad. How old is the current delinquent?'

'Jacky Jacks! Nine, I believe. A cherub to look at, something else under the skin, I'm afraid.'

'The makings of another Tony Carr?' pin-pointed Bony, and was interested by the flash born in the cripple's dark eyes.

'Tony Carr never had a chance, Nat. Jacky Jacks is loved by good parents. There's the difference. My brother George knows that, but he'll never admit it. That was a terrible thing to have happened to him; it was worse than what happened to me.'

The dark eyes peered earnestly into the blue eyes of this man of two races, and the blue eyes detected the pain, and the courage which had been summoned to keep it at bay. Bony said gently:

'Tell me about it.'

'They'd been married four years, Nat. Such a lovely pair. George is ten years younger than I, and she was five years younger than he. They were expecting a baby, the first. We'd been visiting at Kalgoorlie, and I was driving the car home. We could see the other car coming towards us, and I felt something was wrong and steered our car nearly off the road. There were two young chaps in the oncoming car. I could see them laughing. They drove straight at us, playing chicken, so they said afterwards. I was in hospital when they let George tell me that his sweetheart-wife had been killed. And it wasn't my brother George at all, Nat. That feller that just went out isn't my brother George. He will be, for a little while, just while he is trying to drill a little sense into Jack Jacks.'

The acidity had vanished from her voice, and when she

covertly dabbed at her eyes with a handkerchief, Bony asked:

'And how will he do that, Miss Harmon?'

'You'll see, Nat. He'll be waiting at the school when the children come out for the lunch break. I know what he'll do. He has a pair of old handcuffs, and one of them he's made smaller by binding light rope around it. He'll grab little Jacky and put that little cuff on him, and he'll have the other cuff on his own wrist.

'They'll come walking up the street like that, and into the office. Then George will ask his questions and write down all the answers. Then he'll read it out and make the child put his name to it, and glare at the mite with his grey eyes, and take him out and lock him in a cell for about two minutes. And then he'll open the cell and bring the boy back to the office, and talk soft and kind to him, and get him to promise to be good. That's what he'll do I know. I've watched him with other boys. During those few times is when he's my brother as he was before the smash.'

'He's not like that with Tony Carr?'

'Oh no! Tony Carr is dyed in the wool, a chip of the foul block, a brand for the fire. You know, all those old clichés. He's made up his mind that Tony Carr did those murders. The dreadful thing about Tony Carr is that he looks a little bit like the young chap who was driving the car that smashed into us. George and the other officers from Kalgoorlie would have arrested Tony if it hadn't been for Fred Joyce and Melody Sam sticking up for him.'

'And you think that Tony Carr isn't all bad?' prompted Bony pouring himself a cold cup of tea. Surprisingly, she said:

'What d'you think?'

Now he smiled at her, hoping to dispel her mood.

'I asked you first, remember.'

'I don't think he's all bad, Nat. I don't think any boy is all bad, and if he is, he was made bad, and what's been made could be unmade. I don't know how. This strange brother I'm living with has destroyed so much of me. Perhaps it's because he's so

79

right so often. But we have to give everyone the benefit of doubt, haven't we?'

'We should always do so, of course, Miss Harmon.'

Bony rose and moved towards the open door. Pausing, he looked back at the woman, a vast pity surging over him.

'Thank you for the morning tea. I'd like you to invite me again some time.'

She nodded, then said commandingly:

'Come back here.' He returned. 'Sit down again.' He obeyed. Her dark eyes wandered over his face, feature by feature, and fractionally her head nodded as though approving of what she was seeing. 'All right, Nat. You may go now.'

Again outside in the compound where the sunlight was strong and clear, and in which human pain and agony of mind would never exist ... and did ... Bony strolled across to the horse yards, where he bridled and saddled the grey gelding. The horse nickered and danced, and he talked to him, calling him names and whispering threats of what he'd do when they were away from Daybreak.

Several false mounts before the genuine one which found Bony in the saddle, and temper in the mind of the animal at having been tricked. A few rootings, and a smart slap of the rein-end to remind the grey that the end of foolery was now, and then out into the street, where a stately walk was ordered. The council staff leaned on his shovel and waved. Sister Jenks, who was crossing the road, politely waved good-day. And First Constable Harmon might have stopped to admire his equine property were he not on duty escorting a prisoner to the station office for questioning. He was looking straight ahead, and the prisoner was crying without restraint.

CHAPTER 12

The Dreaded Event

As with many out-back hotels, here at Daybreak single male guests occupied rooms in a detached building fronting the main yard, a custom dictated by the necessity of excluding cheque-men and unattached males from the hotel proper; for in their own quarters they could drink, fight, and otherwise enjoy themselves without disturbing other guests and the staff. The yardman occupied one of these rooms.

For Bony the day began at dawn when he stepped from his room, carrying shaving kit and towel, and crossed the yard to the shower block. Like previous days, this one promised to be clear and warm, with a light south wind, and even thus early a gown was not needed. It was five-twenty and the kitchen range had not to be cleaned and re-lit until six o'clock.

He shaved and showered in leisurely manner, and it was fully light, although the sun had not risen, when he left the shower block for his room – and he was a third of the way across the yard, when he halted. There, quite plain, were the tracks of sandshoes size eight, the replica of the tracks he himself had made with Harmon's plaster casts.

The physical suppleness produced by vigorous towelling was replaced by freezing tensity. His eyes narrowed, then blazed wide. His lips pursed to emit a soft whistle, and the nostrils twitched and flared as though trying to smell the man who had left those tracks some time during the night.

The tracks were heading for the fence at the rear of the yard, and they certainly did not pass close to Bony's bedroom door. Instead of following them he backtracked without difficulty, and thus arrived at the side door of the main building, on either side of which were the windows of the bedrooms. From the side door, backtracking led him to the second bedroom window to the right. His hands were twitching, for generations of abor-iginal hunters now controlled him. Gone was the suavity, the mask of white superiority, leaving nothing but elemental man.

He had read the story on the page of the hotel yard.

The man wearing sandshoes, that same man who wore sand-shoes when two persons were murdered, had climbed over the back fence, had crossed direct to this particular bedroom window, had wakened the sleeper and persuaded him or her to open the side door. There at the door had been a struggle, following which the man had retreated to the back of the fence and climbed over it.

And on the other side of that door would surely be the fourth victim.

Bony was halfway on those tracks leading to the fence, when he faltered, halted, brought up by memory of who he was. He was panting, and was ashamed. He was trembling, and was ashamed. Red anger required moments to cool. It was like fighting his way up from the depth of a red fog of ecstasy to the open purity of reason.

Tossing kit and towel in through the doorway of his room, not bothering to dress, he ran across the street and roused Harmon, for Constable Harmon was the representative of Law here and over an area of some half-million square miles. 'Come on. Our man was in the hotel yard last night.'

Such was Bony's command over himself that Harmon re-ceived shock from the words. Also in night attire, he ran with Bony to the hotel yard, and inside the now open gates Bony outlined the murderer's movements, and voiced his conviction of what they would find inside that door.

'Who occupies that particular bedroom?' he asked.

'Don't know,' snapped Harmon. 'Melody Sam sleeps in this end one.' Striding to the side door, he stood looking down at the maze of tracks, and could see none but those made by sand-shoes. 'Hell, if he murderered anyone out here, he must have kept their feet off the ground while he was doing it.'

With forefinger and thumb he was able to turn the door handle without touching the knob, and slowly pushed inward.

Gently the door swung against the inside wall, disclosing a short passage, dim and just barely revealing a dark-clad object on the floor at the angle.

Bony followed the large man to stoop over the woman. She was wearing a blue gown. It was Kat Loader, and superficial examination proved she was dead, and had been dead for several hours.

'Get Sam,' snarled Harmon.

'A moment,' whispered Bony. 'We can't do anything here. We can follow those tracks while they're fresh and before the wind gets up. I'll get Sam, but we mustn't delay here.'

'You've said it, Nat. Go on! Second door on the right.'

Melody Sam was sitting up in bed smoking his first pipe of black tobacco, and he was truly astonished to see Bony walk in on him. Sitting on the edge of the bed, and permitting his expression to give warning of tragedy, Bony began with:

'There's been another killing, Sam. In the hotel. It's your granddaughter. Kat . . . lying out there in the passage. Take it easy. We have to follow the feller's tracks. Came in and went out over the back fence.'

The bedroom blind was lowered, but the risen sun lightened the room. The old man's eyes changed almost to black. Carefully he placed the hot pipe on the ashtray beside the bed. Slowly he nodded understanding, and Bony stood to permit him to lower his feet to the floor. Without a tremor in his voice, he said:

'This time, Nat, I'm goin' to shoot the first detective that enters Daybreak. The useless bastards! You and me'll get that killer, Nat, and we'll hang him feet up under all the other trees. Where is she?'

His feet now in slippers, Melody Sam stood swaying and glaring down at Bony, and Bony said icily:

'You are going to use your noggin, Sam. You will stand by your dead, and I shall track that feller if I have to follow him across an ocean. Now come along. Hold yourself.'

'I can do that, all right, Nat.' Following Bony, he stood for a moment gazing at the dead woman. 'How was it done,

Harmon? Strangled like Mavis Lorelli was. All right, you bastard. We'll lift you up from the ground and let you hang slowly, and ask you how you like it.'

There was a stock inspector staying at the hotel, and he appeared with the cook. To them Harmon gave instructions to stand guard over the body, and, if possible, over the side door handle, which might give prints. Then he and Bony went out into the warming sun, and followed the tracks to the back fence.

Beyond the fence was a goat yard, and beyond that open country. They pushed their way through the flock of goats to the far side of the yard, over the low railings, and again picked up the tracks.

'He went down the slope,' Harmon said, and there could be no mistake, for the tracks of the sandshoes were plain. 'I'd better get a horse. He could be mounted.'

'Hope he is,' assented Bony. 'Horse tracks give us more. You could do with a gun.'

'I'll get both.'

Harmon ploughed his way back through the goats, and Bony renewed his tracking. The murderer had gone directly down the slope. For a thousand yards the tracking was no task whatever, and then the murderer had stepped on to surface rock, as it was known he had previously done. The surface rocks were small in area, and the man could step from one to another, or leap between others. Bony kept on till he reached the lower edge of the rock masses, and there failed to find the tracks of sandshoes. There were boot tracks, the tracks left by barefooted children, but not the murderer's tracks, no tracks made by a man having a slight limp. It meant circling the entire rocky area to find where the sandshoe man had left it.

Time was precious. The sun was gaining height. The wind was shifting to the east. He swore, politely. He had been tricked even thus early.

The killer could not have crossed this large area of individual surface rocks in the dark of night, for, no matter how good his eyesight, there was no difference in colour between rock and ground, or difference in level of rock with the earth.

84

He, Bony, had been tricked by not putting himself into the mind of the fugitive.

Returning to the tracks where they reached the rocky area, he had to scout both south and north to find what the killer had done to thwart his certain trackers. Feeling himself on rock, he had located a low shrub, and had leaped to it, and from it had managed to gain another, and then another. Bony could see the broken plants, which from casual sighting would give the picture of goats having fed on them. The shrubs the killer could see in the dark of the night.

The sandshoe tracks now led Bony to the north and parallel with the town, then slewed on down the slope, and away from the back yards of houses. It now appeared that the killer was making for the mulga forest, or perhaps to the scrub trees, to one of which he had neck-roped a horse.

Again the fellow came to surface rock, but this surface was a continuous mass covering three to four acres, and anyone reasonably familiar with the location could find it in the night. Bony didn't bother to track across it. He proceeded to circle it to find where the man had stepped off it on to trackable earth again. He found the tracks of the man wearing old leather shoes. He had made the change, but he could not disguise the manner of his walk; viz., the distance between strides, the angle of placing the feet, and the limp.

Now he was going up the slope towards the north end of Main Street. Ha! Here he had tripped over an old mulga root, sprawling forward on his hands, and then, on regaining his feet, had rubbed out the handmarks. On again. Now there was something wrong with his walk. Hurt, perhaps? But no, here he was his normal self. Up towards Daybreak; back to Daybreak; back to his lair with the killing lust satisfied, to fall asleep and wake to remember the details as of a dream. So saith the psychiatrist.

Harmon came running down the slope, to gasp that he couldn't wait to locate the butcher's horse as he recalled seeing it loose on the town common.

'How you going, Nat?' he managed to get out.

'Good. Our gentleman changed his sandshoes for leather

ones on that rock back there. Here's his tracks now. He's carrying the sandshoes. Promising, Harmon, very.'

'I hope,' snarled the policeman. 'You sound like Sherlock Holmes already. Where's he making for, back to town?'

'Surely. That's where he lives.'

Now confident of Bony's capabilities, more so because of his colouring than previous proof, Harmon maintained position to the tracker's rear. He had changed into uniform trousers, and about his waist was a leather belt carrying a holster, complete with heavy service revolver. The tracks of the leather shoes or boots led them to the far end of Main Street, and then along that street to enter the side gate of the butcher's premises.

'Thought so,' breathed Harmon.

The lane-way ended at the yard behind Fred Joyce's house and shop. Outside the back door the butcher was emptying a teapot and, seeing them, he became a statue to be titled 'Australian's Daily Chore'. He witnessed Bony, followed by the policeman, advance direct to the hessian doorway of a hut at the yard's far fence.

The hut was on a par with those at Dryblowers Flat, being constructed with wood slabs under a corrugated iron roof. There was glass to the window, but no door. There was a chimney made of sheet iron, which, like the roof, was badly rusted. Outside the entrance several salt-sacks had been sewn together to form a mat.

'It's him, eh?' whispered Harmon, and, almost reluctantly, Bony nodded. Then he was swept aside and Harmon stood before the curtained entrance, feet wide apart, gun drawn.

'You there, Tony Carr?' he called. 'Come outside a moment.'

They heard Tony mumble something which could have been 'All right, Boss.' Then the hessian curtain was moved aside and the lad appeared, wearing old pyjama trousers only. Bony was conscious of Fred Joyce and another man standing with him behind the policeman.

'Come on out, Tony,' commanded Harmon, his voice cold with menace, the gun aimed at the lad's stomach.

'I . . . I didn't kill anybody,' Tony said, amazed.

He moved forward, letting the curtain drop behind him, and Harmon advanced upon him, and with a swift flick of his wrist reversed the revolver and hit him between the brows with the butt. Tony sank down on his knees and covered his face with his hands, and Harmon raised the gun to deal another blow.

'Here, hold it, Harmon!' shouted Joyce, and Harmon found his right arm in a lock, and Bony's breath hot against his neck.

'Drop it, you fool,' snarled Bony. 'Cut that out. We've to find those shoes before you can charge him.'

'I'll kill the murderin' bas . . .'

'I'll break your arm if you don't calm down. Drop it, I say.'

Gradually the frenzy waned in the big man, and the revolver slipped from his hand. Bony kicked it towards Bert Ellis, who was with Joyce. Tony Carr was slumped forward on the ground, his face still cupped in his hands. Bony continued to hold command.

'You take care of Tony, Fred, while Constable Harmon and I search this place for evidence concerned with the murder of Kat Loader.'

'Cor, blimey!' bleated Ellis, and Joyce swore and came to stand beside Tony Carr. 'All right,' he shouted. 'We'll 'tend to Tony.'

The leather boots were on the earth floor at the foot of the bed. They could not locate the sandshoes.

'Them the boots?' asked Harmon harshly of Bony, who was examining their heels and soles.

'Yes,' replied Bony. 'But go easy. It's the sandshoes we want more than these. We must find them. You can only hold Carr on suspicion so far. Better get him over to your office before the crowd gathers. Could be trouble.'

'Smart feller, eh! When I want advice I'll ask for it. I'm wanting those sandshoes at the moment.'

Their search left no possibility of the sandshoes being in the hut. Harmon went outside, followed by Bony. He stood away and stared about. He shouted:

'I want a pair of sandshoes, size eight, the toe of the right one scuffed a bit. They'll be hereabouts. Hunt for 'em. You, Fred, I'm holding you responsible for young Carr.'

He and Ellis and Bony 'scouted' about the hut, and the yard. It was Ellis who found the sandshoes on the flat roof and tossed them down to Bony, and Harmon came and stood close and waited for Bony's opinion. Then he was staring down into those blue eyes which now grew in size and captured him so that he was never to forget them. Beyond the blue eyes he heard the voice.

'These are the shoes which made the prints of which plaster casts were taken, Constable. These could be the shoes which made the prints last night in the hotel yard. Remember you're not the lad's trial jury and judge.'

'To hell with you,' snarled Harmon. He almost knocked Bony aside and went forward to grab Carr by an arm and haul him to his feet. Semi-conscious, Carr was partially carried from the yard and across the street to the police station, followed by Ellis and Fred Joyce.

Bony went back to the hotel and checked the murderer's footprints from the side door to Tony Carr's hut.

CHAPTER 13

A Stirring Day

Five o'clock, and for Daybreak the day had been the fourth of such tremendous days. At five o'clock the population of Daybreak was still divided, one group lingering outside the police station, the other group clinging hard to the hotel. It was expected that within the next hour police and a doctor would arrive from Kalgoorlie.

In the bar Detective-Inspector Bonaparte raked in the money for Melody Sam, and Melody Sam served, with never a word to indicate what was passing through his mind, if anything, for it seemed he was a stunned man. And on the bed in the room she had occupied was the body of Katherine Loader.

Never in this bar had the crowd been so silent. Nothing was said above a whisper, and the sound of comment and discussion was like the ocean heard from a great distance, with that undertone of threat of storm before morning.

It appeared that Harmon had secured his prisoner barely in time to prevent an ugly incident, for Melody Sam had attempted to rouse the people to remove the prisoner from Harmon's custody and exact unimpeded justice. This proposed crime could be excused in view of what the people of Daybreak had been subjected to, plus their isolation in this State of Western Australia.

A beneficial result of the threatened lawlessness had been a severe brake on Constable Harmon, following the unwarranted attack on Tony Carr. That had almost caused Bony to declare himself and exert his authority, and this he would have done, were he fully convinced that Carr was the long-sought murderer.

He found, on his return to the town from the second tracking, that Carr had two friends, one quite unexpected, the other a possibility. The unexpected friend was Bert Ellis, the other the policeman's sister. According to Ellis, when the three of them with the prisoner arrived outside the cell-block, they were met by Esther Harmon. Young Carr was still in bad shape, and she wanted to know what had happened. Ellis had blurted out the truth that without provocation the policeman had dealt a cruel blow with the butt of his revolver. Harmon, having thrust the prisoner inside the cell, was then upbraided by his sister, and he was still in such mental condition that he threatened to lock her up, too, if she didn't return to the quarters.

When she had gone, in her ungainly crippled manner, Harmon had gone to his office for an old and large padlock and with this he double-locked the door bar, and then had ordered Joyce and Ellis to accompany him to the office, to take their statements.

'What happened to Nat?' he asked, his face white and marbled, his eyes unwinking grey-green discs.

'Don't know, George,' replied Joyce. 'I thought he was following us.'

'Gimme that gun,' Harmon said to Ellis, and Ellis was unaware that he was still carrying it. Harmon took the gun, broke it open, blew down the barrel and the chambers, and cleaned it with a rag. Both witnesses were astonished to see that it had not been loaded when used as a club, and now Harmon took a box of cartridges from a desk drawer, and proceeded to load each chamber.

'That young swine was goin' to go for me. You know that,' he said. 'I will expect your cooperation'.

Ellis opened his mouth to refuse, when the butcher cut in with:

'Circumstances a bit unusual, George. Anyway, me and Bert will support you in return for you letting Tony be. Treat him right from now on, OK. Treat him rough, and you'll be out of the Department mighty quick.'

'So you're on his side? Sort of made him your son, eh?'

'Kid's all right, or could have been,' argued Joyce. 'Well, that's how it is with us. You better let Sister Jenks see him. Be your age, George. You got a lot ahead of you.'

Constable Harmon sponged his face with the palms of his hands, and when he looked at them again, his eyes were normal and the strain was leaving his face and shoulders. Ellis was sent for Sister Jenks.

She came, energetic as usual, her voice authoritative.

'Well, Constable Harmon, what is all this about your prisoner?'

'He was hurt in the process of being arrested, Sister. Would you have a look at him?'

Nodding coolly, carrying her medical bag, she followed Harmon to the cell. He flung open the door and stood ready to receive a charge. Nothing like that happened. Tony Carr was sitting on the bunk, his face buried in his hands, the blood from the head wound staining them. She ordered a basin of water.

On bringing the basin, obtained from Esther Harmon, Ellis found the policeman still on guard outside the cell, and Sister Jenks kneeling beside the bunk, on which she had persuaded the prisoner to lie. Ellis held the basin whilst the wound was being cleansed. Nothing was said by anyone until, having dressed the wound and given the patient a couple of tablets, Sister Jenks briskly told the prisoner she would return in an hour. With that, she strode from the cell and the police station, without another word.

Harmon was taking statements from Joyce and Ellis when Melody Sam appeared with the postmaster, and Melody Sam demanded that he, being a Justice of the Peace, immediately try the prisoner for murder, and 'to hell with a jury'. The postmaster objected. Harmon and Joyce eventually pacified Melody Sam and were about to take him back to the hotel, when several men and a number of women appeared, and Sam appealed to them to see that justice was done swift and sure.

'Harmon's got the Daybreak murderer,' he bellowed. 'Daybreak's ours. We got a Justice, we can form a jury if it's necessary, which it isn't.'

Voices supported him, and during the hubbub, according to Ellis, Harmon changed into a man Ellis didn't recognize, not having known him before tragedy soured him.

'And I've got two vacant cells that I'll fill to the brim if you people don't get out of this compound and stay out,' he shouted, with no anger but granite determination in his voice. 'Go on, now. I gotta job, and you're not doing it for me.'

He moved forward as though walking a beat, and flanking him and a little to his rear walked Joyce and Ellis and the postmaster. The crowd turned and walked ahead to the street gate, and out to talk under the nearest pepper tree.

It was then that they missed Melody Sam, and they found him slumped in the policeman's chair at the station office. Sitting on the corner of the desk, Harmon said:

'Sam, you and me have been good cobbers ever since I came to Daybreak. You own Daybreak. I am the Law. You get along back to Daybreak. Both Daybreak and the Law are in West Australia, and the year's nineteen fifty-eight, not eighteen fifty-eight.'

The old man stood and glared at Harmon. Passing round the end of the desk, he patted the policeman on the shoulder, strode to the door, and accompanied by Ellis, went back to his hotel, where he proceeded to serve drinks to the customers who 'flowed' in after them. It was then five to nine.

Under the circumstances, it wasn't possible for Harmon to leave the police station. Soon after he had subdued Melody Sam and sent him back to the hotel, Bony arrived at his office with plaster casts he had made of the sandshoe tracks at the side door, and of those boot tracks close to the entrance to Carr's hut. With these Harmon was happy, went on with his preparations, and twenty minutes later was made happier when Bony arrived with the hotel side door.

'No one touched it, and, as you may not have printing aids, better to have the entire door locked up,' he explained, and only at a later date did Harmon recall this exhibition of efficiency.

Much had happened before five o'clock. Harmon had contacted his Divisional Headquarters and gained agreement on moving his prisoner to Laverton. He had the Justice of the Peace swear in, as special constables, Fred Joyce and a man named Morton. He had permitted Sister Jenks to visit Carr when she came again at ten o'clock. When she left, he asked his sister to provide a meal for the prisoner, saying he would be taking him in his car to Laverton at eleven.

Esther had the prisoner's lunch prepared when her brother entered the kitchen for it. It consisted of cold meat sandwiches and a jug of tea, the sandwiches being in a compact block, and the tea sugared and containing milk. No knife and no spoon, and the food set on white paper on the narrow wood tray.

People knew when escort and prisoner were due to leave, and there was a crowd outside the closed compound gates. Harmon, supported by his specials, entered the cell and handcuffed the prisoner, who was taken to the car, ordered into the seat beside the driver, and a third cuff tethered the cuff on his left wrist to the window bar. Thus he could make the journey in comparative comfort, and be quite unable to attack the driver.

They left exactly at eleven o'clock, the watching crowd being both silent and inactive, and unimpressed by the special constables. And then almost the entire town entered the hotel to celebrate the lifting at long last of a heavy cloud of fear and suspicion; to celebrate, subdued and genuinely sorrowful for old Melody Sam.

Bony had not been out of the hotel since making his plaster casts that morning, and had relied on Bert Ellis to keep him *au fait* with events. This had necessitated many free beers at Sam's expense, and so was a glorious day for the council staff. Between drinks, Ellis imparted his scraps of information in hoarse confidential remarks across the bar counter, and thus Bony knew that after the departure of Harmon with the prisoner, Fred Joyce had driven to the aborigines' camp, and brought Iriti and two other men to check and report on the murderer's tracks from hotel door to Tony's hut.

'Why did Joyce do that, d'you know?' asked Bony.

'Wasn't Fred's idea, Nat. Me and Joyce went with 'em. Foller the tracks easy: Tony's sandshoes, even your seven boots and Harmon's nines. Those rocks would have bluffed me, though. Tony was cunnin' all right. Picked up his boots when he'd changed 'em. Follow them clearly to Main Street, and into the yard to his hut.'

'None of you could have missed, Bert,' Bony said, adding: 'Did the abos say anything of what they saw?'

'Nothing till we got back to the hut. Then Fred asked 'em if they was Tony's tracks, and Iriti grunted a "Yes" and the others backed him up. Fred took them to the police office to get 'em to thumb-print a statement. Got me to sign one too.'

At a quarter to six the customers were watching the clock behind the bar counter.

Everyone knew Harmon's official itinerary arranged with his headquarters. He was to conduct the prisoner to Laverton, where would be waiting police officers and a doctor. Other officers would take over the prisoner and convey him to Kalgoorlie, and Harmon would return to Daybreak with the doctor and detectives.

The state of the road being known, distances assessed, it was voted that Harmon would arrive back at Daybreak at five o'clock, and not later than half past six if he stayed for a meal at Laverton.

A few minutes before six, Melody Sam, without notice of

93

intention, stopped filling glasses, and turned back to the cupboard, where he kept his violin. The crowd ceased speaking and watched. Sam tuned the instrument, tucked it under his chin, and began to play. He moved to the drop-flap in the counter and someone raised it for him to pass through. The crowd parted to give him passage to the front entrance, and remained mute whilst listening to the dwindling music, as Melody Sam moved down Main Street. The tune was 'Love's Old Sweet Song', and without doubt Sam could play it.

Someone said: 'Poor old bastard. Fill 'em up, Nat.'

Following long restraint, comparative uproar arose, and Australia really rocked on beer. Without invitation, Fred Joyce moved behind the counter to assist Bony, and it became obvious that he was as good a barman as he was a butcher. No one heard the clock strike six, and no one noticed the postmaster until he clambered on the counter and demanded to be heard.

'Got some news, gents, got some news,' he shouted, and waited for silence. 'You know the road gate three miles this side of Laverton. Well, Harmon gets out of his car to open the gate. Gets it open, and then is almost run down by his own car. The murderer is out of the handcuffs and driving it. Harmon gets left to walk three miles. And no one's seen the murderer or the car since.'

The announcement was followed by the ticking of the clock, so astonished was the crowd. When the postmaster, perhaps wishing to rush back to his telephone, jumped from the counter and pushed his way to the door, half the crowd followed him into the street. It was an opportunity Bony accepted to close the hotel, promising to open again at eight.

'Keep you going all night as well as all day,' observed Joyce. 'Now what d'you know! That young feller gettin' out of them handcuffs. Don't get it. Must be a proper Houdini or something.'

'They'll grab him soon enough, Fred. Not much of a bushman.'

'Good enough, if he uses his block, to get a long way,' asserted Joyce, now gathering glasses, which Bony proceeded to wash and polish. 'Gosh! To think I was backing him, believing he'd make good! Harmon was right after all. As they start, so they end. And Harmon will be fit for chains after this.'

Joyce stayed to assist Bony to clean up, and then, locking the bar, Bony stood outside the building rolling the first cigarette for several hours. It did seem that every evening at Daybreak was quiet and crowned with peace. There were now very few people on Main Street. Under the trees coming towards the hotel was Melody Sam, accompanied by the minister.

CHAPTER 14

An Opponent for Bony

Melody Sam was the minister's most important parishioner, apart from the fact that Melody Sam was the greatest financial supporter of the Daybreak Church. Melody Sam was apt to rant and roar, and go on a bender in the cellar, but there is always the time when the toughest man is weak and turns to strength, and fortunate is he when there is a Reverend MacBride to whom to turn. The minister brought him back to the hotel, persuaded him to eat, assisted him into bed, gave him a sedative, and consoled him until he fell asleep.

The Reverend MacBride suggested, where another might have commanded, that the hotel be kept closed for that evening at least, and with this Bony, the yardman, agreed and tacked a notice to the bar door reading: 'Shut. By order.' By whose order wasn't of the slightest importance.

At ten o'clock Daybreak waited in retirement. No policeman arrived. Residents sat on the seats around the pepper trees, still discussing the day's events, and the postmaster waited impatiently for news from his opposite number in Laverton, or from homesteads along the road. At nine Bony strolled down the street, crossed to skirt the church, circled wide, and so came to the back fence of the police compound. Finally he was gazing

95

through the unmasked window of the policeman's living-room.

There Esther Harmon was talking with Joy Elder. They were facing each other across the table, and in Joy's left hand was a rumpled handkerchief. Bony knocked on the back door, and it was opened by the girl.

'Why, Nat Bonnar!' she exclaimed, dully. 'Miss Esther, it's Nat.'

'Ask him in, Joy. I've been expecting him.'

'Good evening, Miss Harmon! So, you've been expecting me.' Unsmilingly, Bony crossed to the window and drew down the blind. 'The neighbours, you understand,' he said calmly, and seated himself at the long side of the table. 'No word yet from your brother?'

'As though you wouldn't know,' replied Esther grimly, and Joy broke in with:

'You don't think Tony's the murderer, do you? You can't believe that. I know he isn't. He couldn't be. You found him with me that afternoon, and know he couldn't even bring himself to take out the splinter.'

'I've been telling Joy that it couldn't look blacker against Tony Carr,' interposed Esther Harmon, dark eyes like beads. 'But I don't think he's the murderer, and I've been telling Joy so. The shoes could have been planted on him and all. But . . .'

'Yes, the "but", Miss Harmon. There is the "but". May I smoke?'

'Everyone does without asking me, Nat. Tell us what you came for.'

'Well . . .' Bony slowly rolled the cigarette, and deliberately struck the match and applied the flame. 'I've been wondering about Tony and your brother. Your brother couldn't be called a dill, and Tony Carr is a hefty young feller with strong hands and fairly thick wrists. It would seem that the window bar to which his handcuffs were attached by a spare cuff must have been weak, and that he wrenched himself free from the bar and then gripped the steering-wheel with the cuffs still about his wrist. Don't you think that's how it must have happened?'

'Could be. I don't know, Nat. I haven't thought about it.'

'There is, of course, another picture,' Bony went on, a smile about his mouth which wasn't reflected in his eyes, dark-blue in the lamplight. 'It's likely there was fat along the edges of the meat in the sandwiches you cut for Tony's lunch today. With the fat he could have greased his wrists and be able to work his hands from the cuffs. But even so, that little "but" enters again. Tony's hands and wrists are large, and the police cuffs would surely fit the wrists and leave nothing to spare. You didn't provide anything else with the sandwiches, did you? Or add anything to the jug of tea?'

'I added mustard and salt to the sandwiches, and sugar and milk to the tea.'

'Thoughtful of you, Miss Harmon. But then that is what almost any woman would do. Don't you agree, Joy?'

'Of course. Yes, of . . . but why all this silly talk? Tony got away, and that's the main thing. They'll never catch him. At least I hope so . . . I wish I knew.'

'It would have been very much better for Tony if he hadn't escaped,' Bony said. 'He would have been safe in a nice comfortable cell in Kalgoorlie. Now he'll be hunted like a rabbit. And Constable Harmon is going to come home a very angry man. And if Tony didn't gain freedom by wrenching away the window bar, then Constable Harmon is going to ask a lot of questions in a nasty manner.'

'Such as, Nat?' challenged Esther.

'Such as, when addressing himself to his special constables, who assisted him to remove Tony from the cell to the car, demanding to know which of them passed to the prisoner a spare key to the handcuffs.'

'Well, if that was how it happened, I hope George takes it out of them, Nat. A policeman has enough to do without people giving handcuff keys to prisoners. Now you answer my questions.'

'With pleasure. And when you've done. I'll ask you some more.'

'How is Melody Sam making out?'

'Sound asleep. Sister Jenks plus Mr MacBride fixed that.'

'And the hotel closed, or you wouldn't be here. Who's over there beside the cook and that Kalgoorlie girl who's the maid now?'

'No one else when I left. The two women ought to be all right. They've locked themselves in, and besides, the murderer is caught, isn't he?'

'No, he isn't,' protested both women in unison, the elder vehemently, the young tearfully. Joy Elder's reaction Bony could understand. They knew that Kat Loader had been lured to that side door, and, before she could step from the portal to the soft sandy ground, had been caught by the murderer's hands and killed when her naked feet were clear. The main argument in favour of Tony's innocence was that he didn't have the strength to do just that.

Aware that the feminine mind will seek any prop to maintain a preconceived notion, Bony proceeded with them along their road, and had to admit that they were not entirely without logic when Esther Harmon said:

'You men make me tired. You're all like children singing a nursery rhyme. Now be your age, Nat. There's Kat Loader. You knew her better than you know me. Without taking into account that she wasn't a lightweight woman for any man to hold up by the neck like a chook, can you imagine her leaving her bed for someone who knocks on her window, and going to the side door to meet him, unless she knows him extra well?'

'Go on,' invited Bony.

'Thank you. You're not telling us that Kat Loader was so friendly with Tony Carr that she'd open the side door in the middle of the night to gossip with him. Whoever that man is, he was on a better footing with her than that. As good a footing as, say, you, Nat Bonnar. If that's your name, which I doubt.'

'It's one of them,' admitted Bony. 'Have you forgotten that Mary, the maid at the Manse, also went outside to meet the man who murdered her, and who must have been well known to her?'

'I haven't forgotten, Nat. Where were you at that time?'

'Away across in Queensland. Can prove it, too. What say

someone makes a pot of tea? I've been here nearly an hour, and no one has proved to be very hospitable.'

'Make a pot of tea, Joy,' said Esther, and to Bony: 'Can't rile you, can we? One of these days I'm going to take you to pieces to find out how you breathe. D'you believe Tony Carr is the murderer?'

'I followed the tracks of the man who killed Kat Loader,' Bony replied sternly. 'The tracks led me to rock where that man changed his sandshoes for boots, and the boot tracks led me to Tony Carr's shack. The sandshoes were on the roof, and the boots were at the foot of his bunk. Tony Carr walks like the man who wore the sandshoes and the boots. The black trackers who followed those tracks say the same thing.'

'You're not answering my question,' objected Esther, and Joy Elder paused with the teapot in her hands, and held her breath.

'Which was?' mildly countered Bony.

'Do you, or do you not, believe that Tony Carr murdered Kat Loader?'

'Sister, I cannot tell a lie. I cut down the pine tree.'

'Joy, throw that pot at him,' commanded the policeman's sister.

Joy Elder dropped the metal teapot to the table and ran to clutch Bony by the arms.

'Don't fool around, Nat. Don't keep on like that. Tell us! Go on, tell us!'

'Of course I don't believe Tony did it,' Bony told her gently, and felt no embarrassment when she clung to him and wept. 'It's why I'm so sorry that someone gave him the key to the handcuffs and so let him escape, when he ought to be in a nice warm jail until all this nastiness is over. Actually, Joy, you should scold Miss Harmon for planting the handcuff key among the sandwiches she cut for Tony.'

'How did you know about the key?' asked the girl, looking up into the blue eyes now so benign in the brown face. Bony, gazing past her at the crippled woman, clashed with defiance in eyes as steady as his own.

'Brain, just brain power,' answered Bony lightly. 'We leave

99

here and find the street outside wet, and so we know it rained. Cause and effect. Tony frees himself from the window bar and drives the car through the gate obligingly opened by Constable Harmon. That was an effect, the cause being a key which unlocked his handcuffs. There must have been a key, because only the other day I was talking with Constable Harmon when he was in the car, and I tested that window bar without conscious reason.'

'Doesn't follow that I gave Tony the spare key,' insisted Esther Harmon. 'Do make that tea, Joy. The kettle's boiling its spout off.'

Bony sat at the table and rolled a cigarette, a man exposed to the inexplicable workings of the female mind. He said:

'Miss Harmon, don't you realize even now that your act could have resulted in tragedy? That either your brother or his prisoner might have been killed? There could have been a fight in the car. The car could have been wrecked. Or your brother . . . he was armed with a revolver, and entitled to use it.'

'Wouldn't have been any good to him, Nat. I took the bullets out before he left.'

'You did what?' Bony sat back, poise almost unseated. He retired to colloquialism. 'Go on, tell me more.'

Esther Harmon moved in her chair, lifting the crippled leg with her hands, nodded to Joy to bring cups and saucers from the cabinet, and smiled sweetly at Bony.

'Very well, Nat, I'll tell you something more. No one knows my brother but me. He's a good policeman, the sort of policeman needed for these outback stations. He knows the Book, and he's able to balance the Book with the character of the people he's got to deal with, and live with, too. That accident you know about burned a blot on his mind, just a little blot making him hate lads round about Tony Carr's age. That's why he hit Tony with his revolver. Not because he suspected of murder, but because he is the same age, and the same type of lad that killed his wife and did this to me.

'I'll tell you more, as you asked for it. No one knows Tony Carr but me. No one, Nat, no one at all. I know all about him from the time he was born. I know all about his beatings, all about his crimes; and all about the crimes committed against him. I know all about the hurts, all about the insults by ignorant people who imagine they themselves are spotless.

'So there are the two of them, both strong, and, as you might say, both a little wrong in the head, hating each other like ordinary people could never do. My brother didn't have to take Tony down to Laverton. He asked Headquarters to let him, and he persuaded whomever he was talking to down there in Kalgoorlie. I knew then that he would pin Tony to that window bar, and what he would be doing to Tony with his tongue all the way, and perhaps with his fists, too. I had to give the boy a chance, so I put the spare key in between the sandwiches with a little note telling him what to do, and when. And, as I told you, I took the bullets out of my brother's revolver. To make those two men equal.'

To make them equal! Bony thanked Joy for the cup of tea she placed before him, and said to Esther Harmon:

'And so young Carr freed himself from the cuffs when your brother was opening the road gate, and then tried to run your brother down in the gateway?'

'That I'll never believe,' Esther retorted. 'I told Tony not to harm George because George is my brother. No one knows those two like I do. And if you go on sitting there like that, just watching me like a kooka-burra on a tree watching a snake, I'll know you like no one else does.'

'Then I'll leave at once,' Bony returned, lightly. 'Before I do, tell me how you know that Tony Carr didn't murder Kat Loader.'

'I will, if you'll tell me why you know he didn't.'

'I know he didn't, well, just because I know he didn't, Miss Harmon.'

'That's how it is with me, Nat.'

'Miss Harmon, I don't believe you.'

'Nat, I don't believe you, either. Hark!' In the ensuing silence they could hear the murmur of an approaching car. 'That'll be George. Out with you, Nat. You too, Joy. Out the back way.'

Bony continued to sit, now shaking his head doubtfully, and

Esther Harmon read his mind at that moment, and smiled, grimly, saying:

'You needn't worry, Nat, I can manage George. Go quickly. He'll be here in five minutes.'

CHAPTER 15

A Feather Bed for Tony

Constable Harmon was accompanied by Inspector Mann, Detective-Sergeant Wellings, and young Doctor Flint, all of Kalgoorlie. Daybreak received the party with blank silence, most all the inhabitants lurking in the abysmal gloom beneath the pepper trees. They had watched the car coming along the back of Bulow's Range, saw its headlights bathe with brilliance the stone image of Melody Sam, chuckled when the party gathered outside the main door of the hotel and someone struck a match to read the notice: 'Closed. By Order.'

'What the hell!' murmured Inspector Mann. ''Tisn't Sunday, is it?'

'Thursday when we left Kal this morning,' claimed Sergeant Wellings. 'What's to do, Harmon?'

'Ruddy soon find out,' exploded Harmon, and proceeded to pound on the door. 'Shut. By Order! What a tale to tell in Daybreak!'

They could hear feet scuffing over the linoleum of the passage beyond the door, which had been built long before egg-box architects designed houses of glass and slats in hot Australia. They heard a heavy bolt being eased, and witnessed the door opening, to reveal the barman holding aloft a kerosene lamp, and arrayed in skyblue pyjamas.

'Police here,' snarled Constable Harmon. 'What's the meaning of this notice?'

'What it says,' replied Bony. 'Place is closed. By Order.'

'Closed my . . . foot.' Harmon argued, and proceeded to wave

Bony back as he advanced, followed by the party. 'Light up, Nat. The inspector and the sergeant and the doctor require accommodation and refreshment. Where's the licensee?'

'In his room. The Reverend put him to bed, and the Sister provided a sedative. Shock, and all that. Mr Loader put me in charge. Said the hotel was to be closed. Said I had to provide refreshment. We have cold goat and bread and butter. And tea. The stock belongs to the licensee, and he isn't compelled by law to dispense it to any traveller. So he said. There's plenty of vacant rooms.'

'What a pub!' moaned the doctor, and the sergeant groaned and waited on the inspector to voice comment.

'What's your name?' asked the inspector, and Bony gave his alias. 'All right, Nat. Light up and get us a cold snack. Don't bother to make tea. You'd like to see the body, Doctor?'

'I don't like seeing bodies at any time,' the doctor said as though he meant it. 'I'll examine it now, of course.'

Bony called for the cook, and lit the ceiling lamps. The cook appeared in her dressing-gown, and, not forgetting the power of cooks in general, Bony politely suggested she might set a light supper-table for the late guests. He indicated Melody Sam's room, and repeated the bulletin concerning his health, asking for reasonable quietness. The sergeant snorted. Constable Harmon glared. The inspector looked vacant.

They all entered the dead woman's room, were there fifteen minutes. Bony then showed them to the bedrooms and the bath-room, and he was waiting, now dressed, in the dining-room when they sought refreshment.

'Look, Nat,' said the doctor. 'We're perishing. What about opening up?'

'Certainly, sir. What'll it be?'

They named their drinks, and even Harmon, who ate with them, relaxed a little. Bony heard them discussing a plan of operations, which was to remain in abeyance until daylight the following morning; and shortly after that, Harmon left for his own quarters.

It was past one o'clock when Inspector Mann requested a few moments of the barman's attention in his room.

The inspector was over six feet tall. His cranium was long and narrow, crowned by sparse black hair machined very short. He was next for promotion to superintendent, the senior officer of the Goldfields District of Western Australia. At this time he controlled the Northern Division of the Goldfields District, and had he 'arrived' fifty or sixty years earlier, there would now be fewer wealthy families living in and about Perth, whose fortunes were founded on gold-stealing.

An expert on gold, its recovery, uses and illicit markets, Inspector Mann would have succeeded in any calling, because of ability to recognize his own limitations. It was why he felt no jealousy of Bonaparte, when, he having failed to locate the murderer of three persons at Daybreak, this expert bush investigator was seconded from Queensland. These two hunters now sat on the edge of the bed, the better to converse without possibility of being overheard.

'Not so cut and dried as Harmon believes, eh?' opened Mann, filling a pipe which should have been incinerated a generation ago. 'Your remaining on the job points to it, anyway.'

'Daybreak is an oyster which can be opened only by the oyster itself,' Bony said. 'To carry the simile further, if the oyster is transferred from salt to fresh water, it will open without outside force. I have changed the water.'

'You don't think young Carr is the man we want?'

'I'm sure he is not.'

During a full minute Inspector Mann merely sucked noisily on his pipe before asking:

'Mind telling me why? This is your assignment. We know how you work, and I have neither desire nor intention of interfering with you or your methods. You'll grant me, however, a degree of curiosity when you permitted Harmon to arrest a man you believe is innocent.'

'Being sure that one man is innocent doesn't prove that another is guilty. Had I stepped forward to prevent Harmon arresting the wrong man, the right man, like my oyster, would have remained closed up for a very long time, perhaps always. I have no proof of who he is. I have evidence that he has carefully

built up spurious evidence against Carr. The arrest and deten-
tion of Tony Carr is a factor I had to accept as the lesser of two
evils, the major evil being the escape of a multiple killer.'

'I see your point. Well, what clears Carr?'

'You have the reports of the trackers, and they all agree that
the man is about 160 pounds in weight, has an eight foot, and
walks with a slight limp. And that he is a white man. You
agree?'

'Yes. Go ahead. You're the oyster now, about to open up a
bit, I hope.'

'I have a reason for opening up a little to you. First however,
this tracking of the man who killed again last night. I tracked
him from the side door, over the back fence, to rock faces and
then to a large area of surface rock where he changed his sandshoes for old boots. Now up to this point it was obvious that
either the aboriginal trackers engaged on the previous cases
were semi-trained, or the killer, after this last killing, intentionally made subsequent tracking of himself comparatively
easy, I think for the purpose of inculpating Carr in this his final
step to his goal. Follow me?'

Inspector Mann nodded, his forgotten pipe cold, but smelly
none the less.

'He walked off the rock and headed diagonally up the slope
to the far end of Main Street. He had covered approximately a
hundred yards when he tripped over an old mulga root which
sent him sprawling. He was careful to erase the marks of knees
and hands, but did nothing about the displaced root.

'As with any other man who trips like he did, he was mentally upset by the incident. He had planned with cunning care
of details. He had murdered with cold calculation. He had
purposely left tracks to indicate carelessness and/or the am-
ateur, as could be expected of Tony Carr's limited experience.
Then he fell over a root in the dark, and the calmness of mind
was replaced by anger. From the root he made a hundred and
twenty-seven steps without limping. Anger caused him to
forget to limp. When making those steps he forgot to walk like
Tony Carr does, the lad having suffered a genuine physical
injury.'

Inspector Mann sighed, nodded, grinned, remembered his pipe and struck a match. Over the agitated flame he regarded Bony.

'There's no ruddy doubt, Bony, that you have the know-how,' he said, and placed the burned match back in the box. He asked no probing questions, able to see the inference and evaluate them without doubting this man of two races. 'What a bastard! Planning to murder maybe half a dozen people to reach some place in his overall scheme, and tie the lot on a known juvenile criminal.'

'You will recall that I mentioned I had a reason for confiding in you,' Bony went on. 'That reason concerns young Carr. I understand he escaped from Harmon.'

'Easy. Just slipped the cuffs when Harmon was opening a road gate. Gate nicely opened, and he drove through. Tried to run Harmon down.'

'Slipped the cuffs!'

'Yes. Car found out of petrol beyond Laverton, which he by-passed. Probably thumbed a lift to Kalgoorlie.' Mann chuckled. 'Could have been on either of two trucks, or in one of three cars which passed us before we reached Laverton.'

'Harmon was doubtless annoyed,' observed Bony, keeping his gaze to the task of rolling a cigarette, and joyful that Esther Harmon would not be tackled about the spare key. She had relied on the boy not to harm her brother, and he hadn't tried, no matter what Harmon said. Carr had gone to the limit to protect her, by re-locking the cuffs after he was free of them.

'Annoyed!' echoed Mann. 'Harmon was frothing at the mouth.'

'And now every member of the Department will be looking for Carr.'

'Naturally.'

'Yes, naturally,' repeated Bony, and stared up into the black eyes above the pipe. 'You will issue a secret instruction that no harm is to come to that lad in any effort to take him.'

'I'll countermand the order to take him.'

'No, you won't. He has to be arrested, and he has to be held. And once you lock him up you'll see to it that he's fed on bacon and eggs, and T-steaks and onions and plumduffs, and that he's given the best cigarettes and provided with the books he chooses. And a soft bed in a cell to himself.'

'You gone wonky?' inquired Mann, mildly.

'You are going to re-arrest an innocent man,' Bony continued. 'You will issue a Press item to the effect that you are holding a man in connection with the Daybreak murders. You do not repeat to anyone what I've told you about those tracks. Before you leave Daybreak, as soon as possible in the morning, you will have from me two letters. One, a confidential report to your Commissioner, and two, a letter to Carr to be given him when you grab him, telling him he's to behave until his Daybreak friend, Nat, uncovers the swine who has framed him. Clear?'

'As pea soup.'

'At all costs, the murderer is not to suspect that his frame is doubted. Is that clear?'

'As distilled water. Blimey, what about a drink?'

'I'll get you one. What do you sip?'

'Sip! Two double Scotches.'

Bony brought a bottle of whisky, there being a water carafe and glasses on the washstand.

'We must keep our voices down,' he said. 'The doctor's next door. Say when.'

'Tomorrow will do. It's on the house?'

'Keep your mind on business, and the house will take care of itself. I'm owed about sixty pounds by the house.'

'Bets or wages?'

'Wages as barman and secretly hired private eye. Have to earn my salary as an employee of the State, though, so you might cooperate to the extent of supplying me with a dossier on Melody Sam.'

'Easy. He's an antique, a character, a history, a ruddy legend. Any particular angles?'

Bony pondered, or Inspector Mann thought he did. He noticed that Bony's whisky would not cover a lump of sugar. He found no need to rack his mind to recall items of intelligence which had come to him concerning this blue-eyed, brown-complexioned man, who like old Melody Sam, was a legend too. Strangely enough, one seldom found these legends in a city. It must be the flaming bush that did things to certain men, making some and destroying others, and ignoring those whose ambition was merely to amass money.

'I'll like to know more of Melody Sam,' Bony said. 'With emphasis on his early years. You know, any falls from grace, such as skulduggery, associations with the aborigines, marriages and children, and the like. Then . . . wait!'

The inspector waited, and poured himself another drink.

'Not so long ago, someone dealt me a card whose value I failed to recognize until Kat Loader was murdered. Now it's been promoted to an ace. Yes, Mann, you send me that dossier on Melody Sam.'

CHAPTER 16

No Foulness on our Hands

Morning came to Daybreak to awaken Melody Sam to consciousness of death and grief and rage. He sat up on his bed, reached for his pipe and tobacco, and when he saw Bony sitting on the edge of the bed he realized how old he was, and how like a rock this stranger from the bush had become.

'How are you feeling?' Bony asked. 'Better?'

'All right, Nat. That sleep done me good. How's the world?'

'Still spinning, Sam. I've brought a tea tray. There are matters to talk about. We had late guests. Harmon came back with Inspector Mann, Sergeant Wellings, and Doctor Flint. You've met Mann before.'

'And that sergeant-detective. Flint's a stranger. What else?'

'The inquest will be held this morning. Probably be adjourned to Kalgoorlie. Young Tony Carr slipped his handcuffs and escaped from Harmon. Happened three miles this side of Laverton. They haven't caught up with him.'

'Hope I do, Nat. I'd give all I have to catch up with him.' The old man stretched his long body, and thumped the cup on its saucer down upon the table, spilling the tea. His grey eyes sparkled and emotion became something like an embattled adversary. 'Young Kat never did anything to harm him. No one here in Daybreak ever did anything wrong against him.'

'You're barking up the wrong tree,' Bony said swiftly.

'I am? What d'you mean by that?'

'I'm not saying until you calm down, Sam. Remember putting me on that extra job as private investigator into these murders?'

'Yes. I'll pay what I owe. I always pay my debts.'

'You haven't sacked me yet. Not from that particular job.'

'Job finished when they arrested young Carr.'

'The job doesn't finish until they arrest the murderer of your granddaughter, and those other victims, Sam. The murderer is still here in Daybreak, which is why I'm asking you to put off your anger like you'll be putting off your nightshirt in a minute or two. The police will be clearing out of Daybreak before noon, and then you and I will have this murderer all to ourselves. That is, if you'll play along.'

Melody Sam took up the saucer, and slurped down the tea spilled into it, drained that in the cup and proffered the cup for a re-fill. Bony could see the effort required to gain mastery over emotion, and did not speak until Melody Sam loaded his pipe and ignited the tobacco.

'That's better,' he said. 'Do we team up?'

'How can I pull me weight, Nat?'

'By not pawing the ground and neighing, and busting your heart trying to move the load all by your little self. In other words, by using your block, being your age, and playing for a rise.'

'Tell me some more,' demanded Melody Sam.

'I don't barter,' Bony said, abruptly chilly. 'I want your promise to play along with me. Or I play it alone. Well?'

'You win, Nat. I'd like to know who I'm playing with, that's all. You can break in horses, but you're no breaker by trade. What do I do?'

'In a couple of minutes you get out of that nightshirt and dress and take over the command of this hotel. You act normally. You tell the cook what to cook, you tell me to earn my money as the yardman. You count the money in the till, and deal with that. You will be asked to identify the body and attend to the funeral arrangements. Afterwards you'll open the bar, as per usual. And what I tell you now, you will keep strictly under your hat. Do you agree?'

The old man nodded.

'As you mentioned, I am not a horsebreaker by trade,' Bony conceded. 'I am, however, by trade a tracker. We talked about tracks the other afternoon, and about the lack of details supplied by the aborigines. It was why you decided to employ me as your private investigator, remember?

'This time yesterday morning I tracked the man who murdered your granddaughter. Later in the morning I tracked him again, to be sure of my first reading. That man, Sam, isn't Tony Carr. That man planted the sandshoes he wore, and the old boots he wore; the boots in Carr's hut and the shoes on the roof. I didn't tell Harmon what I knew because I want the murderer to think he succeeded in framing Tony. Even now he's thinking what a clever feller he is.'

Melody Sam filled his lungs with air, squared his great shoulders and released the imprisoned air as though he'd risen from a deep dive.

'You wouldn't tell me how you knew by them tracks that Tony didn't make 'em?' he suggested.

'No.'

'Oh!' The negative answer had been given with such finality that Melody Sam offered no attempt to upset it. Quietly he said: 'All right, Nat. You're the boss.'

Satisfied with his victory, assured that Melody Sam would not behave irrationally and possibly begin another of his famous benders when it was so necessary that he continue to behave normally, Bony left him to dress, and departed to perform his early-morning chores.

The hotel awoke to the business of another day, and the town stirred to take immediate interest in events which had become repetitious. The yardman cut the cook's daily supply of firewood, then polished the linoleum along the passages, and finally cleaned out the bar and the lounge. Bedroom doors opened, and the showers swished as the guests made their toilets. The breakfast bell was rung, and Bony ate his in the kitchen and chatted with the cook.

At ten o'clock the yardman was called to the police station to give his statement in detail of the tracking he had done in company with Constable Harmon, and his actions on their arrival outside Carr's hut. The inquest wasn't opened, and the doctor signed his certificate. He and the police party left Daybreak shortly before two, leaving Harmon again the officer in charge, and the townspeople free to accompany the funeral cortège to the cemetery.

With the exception of two people, every man, woman and child living at Daybreak, at Dryblowers Flat, and at the homesteads within sixty miles of Daybreak were on Main Street when Katherine Loader passed for the last time under the pepper trees, the casket on the tray of a utility, and bearing but one wreath, comprising all the flowers to be gathered in the township. Behind the utility walked Melody Sam, accompanied by the minister, Fred Joyce and his wife, and followed by the entire population . . . on foot.

Only two people were not of that procession . . . Bony and Esther Harmon. In the silence of the deserted town Bony found her sitting on the front veranda of the station house.

'He said nothing about Tony,' she told him when he sat on the veranda edge almost at her feet.

'Nothing about that key?'

'No. He'll be saving it up, Nat. He's like that.'

'You haven't been told, then, that Tony merely slipped his hands through the cuffs and left them cuffed to the window bar?'

'He did?'

'What do you think?'

'Oh, Nat, I knew he'd do it right for my sake. He must have

unlocked the cuffs, and then re-locked them all in a flash, so that no one would know about that key. What else do you know?'

'That he by-passed Laverton, and drove on for five or six miles before the petrol gave out, and the police think he must have thumbed a ride to Kalgoorlie. You know, Esther Harmon, when it's all summed up, you are a wicked woman. And a very lucky one.'

The dark, almost black eyes deepened as the mind behind them sought to reach his own, and was defeated. She suffered no feeling of frustration, although mystified by something in him which previously she hadn't detected. As with Melody Sam, and with all those others in Daybreak who had encountered the hotel yardman, she had sensed only what he had decided she should do, but now, as Melody Sam had done early this morning, she realized that this man was no itinerant bushman.

Intentionally she moved her crippled leg, and said:

'A wicked woman, and a lucky one, Nat?'

'Wicked because you created grave risk for either or both men in that car. Lucky because your judgement of Tony Carr proved to be correct. Lucky, too, because when that accident happened much was taken from you, but much more was given to you.'

He stood, and now her lips were trembling, and with no further word he turned and left her.

The sunlight was bright and the pepper-tree shadows were dark, and all the town seemed hushed. Frail wisps of cloud beneath the sky of pale blue told of the peace of autumn, when the winds are so gentle that the willy-willies never rise to stagger over this land having no limits. Bony walked out beyond the stone man, and tarried when clear of the street to watch the compact mass of people gathered in the distant cemetery. There, this kindly day, a murderer would be watching his victim being planted in the dust.

Bony wandered back to the hotel, which he entered by the kitchen door. The silence of emptiness greeted him and, having shut and locked the door, he passed to the long passage skirting the dining-room, and so came to the bedrooms. Evidence of the recent guests had been removed, and the doors of those rooms were open. He entered the bedroom long occupied by Kat Loader.

The spirit of Kat lingered here. The fragrance of her he had first encountered when they pretended courtship to entice Melody Sam up from his gelignite den met him again in this room, and aroused that horror and fury he always felt when hunting a killer.

He spent several minutes in the room, looking at the framed photographs on the mantel over the fireplace which was never used, and the three seascapes which would be a Mecca for a woman living all her life so far from the ocean. The dressing-table appointments were decidedly costly, and the lounging-chair by the window was most inviting. Here, a woman had indulged her taste for the best that money could buy.

Melody Sam's room possessed a different odour, the smell of strong tobacco which nothing less than complete renovation would defeat. Bony had, of course, been in this room as recently as that morning, but now he had the leisure to examine it. Compared with the other, it was austere in its furnishings and appointments. There was a vast American roll-top desk. On shelves of plain deal backed by one long wall were five old violins, lumps of quartz wired with gold, specimens of ore in the shape of ancient churches and Eastern palaces, all brought up from Sam's Find. There were nuggets of pure gold, and pieces of a theodolite, old books and wads of documents weighted with gold nuggets. There in a corner stood a safe so vast it was surprising that the floor carried its weight.

The picture over the fireplace was the item Bony really wanted to examine. He raised the window blind and fixed the curtains to provide more light. Enclosed by an ornate gilt frame, it was an enlargement inexpertly coloured, a photograph taken long ago, when gentlemen wore fancy waistcoats and combed their forelocks to dampened quiffs.

There sat Melody Sam, and nothing which the enlarger and the artist had done to the original picture could detract from a face chipped from red granite, or from the power of eyes beneath the beetling brows. Behind him were a man and a woman, obviously Sam's son and his wife. On each side of him

113

stood a little girl, both in the vicinity of seven and eight years of age, and Melody Sam could never deny that these were his grandchildren, for both took after their father, and the son was the incarnation of his father.

Bony left the room and sat on the form outside the bar window and rolled a cigarette. He could see Esther Harmon still meditating on her veranda. A dog lying under a pepper tree stood and uttered a half-hearted bark, wagged his tail and trotted past the stone man; and presently appeared Melody Sam walking home in company with the minister, and after them, forming a ragged procession, came the crowd. Constable Harmon broke away to return to his station. Fred Joyce and his wife reached the sidewalk and passed Bony without glancing at him. Bert Ellis winked as he passed with a tall woman, and in the wink was the aching thirst for a cold beer multiplied by six. Les Thurley, the postmaster, and his wife and all the others passed along the street, leaving Melody Sam to thank the Reverend Mr MacBride for his kindness and help, before sinking wearily to the form beside his yardman.

Moodily watching the retiring minister, Sam said:

'Well, that's that. When's it going to be our turn, Nat?'

'Could be soon. Could be late. It will come,' replied Bony. 'Planting those shoes on Tony gives the man we want a lead, a big lead. Patience, Sam. He's like a mouse in its hole, and I am the cat waiting outside.'

'You know who he is, don't you?' grumbled Sam.

'I do. I've seen his tracks on Main Street. Yes, I know him, but Sam, what I know wouldn't justify Harmon arresting him.'

'I believe you, Nat. Just you give him to me.'

Bony turned slightly towards the patriarch.

'Sam, look at me. I am much younger than you. Had your son lived he would have been about my age. Your son would have said what I am going to say. The age of feuding is past, and I don't think the world is any sweeter for its passing. I am a primitive, as you are. I like simplicity in living, and in common justice . . . as you do. But you and I are out of step with the men and women of today. We have to live in the world they have made, not the world we would have made. We catch that mouse and hand it over to the representative of this other world, the world that is, and when we do hand it over to Constable Harmon, we must be able to describe that mouse, its shape, weight, colour, tracks and actions, and we go on living, Sam, and find no foulness of his blood on our hands.'

CHAPTER 17

Bony Smells the Mouse

The way of a cat with a mouse can be profitable to the student of human psychology.

The cat, strolling along the wainscot, sniffs at a hole, is assured that the mouse is within, and settles into a coma of patience. The mouse, being a natural fidget, cannot bear inactivity and, when not asleep, he must adventure. Knowing that the cat has sniffed him, and unable to adopt complete repose, he must see just what the cat is doing.

In the room the cat has become a fixture, alike with the legs of a table, a chair, a what-not. A squeak of defiance, a rodential ya-hoo, have no more effect on the cat than on the furniture.

Thus the mouse begins that gradual mental process towards the state of regarding familiar things with contempt. As he surveys the outside from deep within, confidence swiftly strengthens and the mouse draws ever nearer to the entrance of his abode, until eventually he is crouching with his head outside the hole, squeaking and winking at the cat.

The cat remains a fixture. The fidget retires for a while before again taking a mouse-eye view from his hole. Nothing has changed. Wariness of danger wears thin. Familiarity drugs thought and begins to blur instinct. At every visit to his doorway the mouse ventures farther out, until all of him is outside save his tail.

So the foolish one continues to ultimate destruction. Once

the mouse has emerged so far that the tip of his tail is no longer inside the hole, he cannot flick himself backward, but must turn about to retreat head first. The turnabout action requires time. Until this fraction of a second, time has meant nothing to the cat; to the mouse it is fatal.

Much of the cat's psychology had been bequeathed to Inspector Bonaparte by his aboriginal mother, a member of a race which down the ladder of the centuries had had to cultivate feline patience if it were to survive.

The death of Katherine Loader proved that the human mouse was still in Daybreak, and now the human cat had sniffed him to his hole. Provided that the cat did not act out of feline character by moving even as much as a whisker, inevitably the moment would come to take the mouse, hide and all.

The next morning Bony completed his usual kitchen chores and then exercised his muscles with the axe at the wood-heap. In the street were sounds of activity. During the night the transport from Laverton had arrived and was parked outside the hotel. Sam was now rousing the truckers, who had merely rolled into their swags beside the tarpaulin-covered loading, and the postmaster was anxious to take delivery of the mail-bags.

After breakfast Sam checked the cases and cartons and drums of beer down the steps to Bony, who stacked the goods in the bar cellar. The remainder of the morning Bony was busy in the bar, Sam having decided to visit the manager of his general store and watch the goods being checked in there. At midday the truck left on the return trip to Kalgoorlie, and Melody Sam took over the bar.

This morning all of Daybreak had been absorbed by the unloading of the truck and the delivery of mail and papers, and so it wasn't until crossing the police compound that Bony smelled another mouse, seeing there the animal's tracks. The scent lay across the compound to a shed where were kept bags of wheat for Esther Harmon's chooks, and lucerne for her brother's horse.

Coming now from this shed was Esther Harmon carrying a

basket. She had apparently been collecting hens' eggs, and on Bony looking into her basket he counted five.

'Goodday, Miss Harmon! Hoping to reach yesterday's tally?'

'I am always hoping to beat the day before, Nat,' she said, brightly. 'Are you going riding?'

'Yes. Your brother is so pleased with himself he gave me permission to take his horse any time I wanted to. Is he about?'

'No. I think he went down the street to speak to the minister. Something to do with a report on Tony Carr.'

'And how is Tony this morning?'

'Why! How on earth . . . Are you trying to be funny, Nat?' The dark eyes glowed angrily, but anger was but a shadow masking alarm.

'Tony must have come back on the truck, under the tarpaulin,' he said. 'He crossed the yard and hid in the feed shed. I think I may assume that you have been talking to him.'

Her finely-moulded mouth trembled, and her hands shook so that he took the basket from her. Bony asked when had she learned that Tony was hiding in the shed.

'After breakfast, Nat. I was gathering the eggs. The hens lay in there. And Tony spoke to me. Nat, you mustn't say anything. We must give him a chance. We can't let him be hunted like a dingo. You won't . . . you won't tell George?'

'It shall be a secret. But why come back here?'

'He said there is nowhere else to go,' Esther explained. 'Said if I wouldn't help him there was no one else he could ask. He was sitting in George's car with the petrol all gone, and when he saw the truck coming, he hid behind a tree. When the men were looking to see whose car it was, he climbed up on the truck and under the tarpaulin. He says he knew it was the Daybreak truck.' They had arrived now at the kitchen door, and she clasped his arm impulsively. 'What are you going to do, Nat? You can't give him up.'

'Have you taken food to him?' Bony asked, and she nodded. 'Then he'll be all right for a while. Your brother is unlikely to go to the shed, and meanwhile we'll think of something. I'll call in on you when I return from my ride.' Patting her shoulder, he said: 'Once I told you you were a wicked woman. I take that back. And with it, half the load you've been carrying since breakfast.'

Collecting the gear from the harness shed, Bony made ready to saddle the gelding, decided to make it easier to catch the animal with a handful of lucerne, and entered the fodder shed. Additional to bales and bags was much discarded junk, all providing Tony with adequate concealment.

'It's all right, Tony,' Bony remarked conversationally, 'I've been talking with Miss Harmon about you. You are to stay where you are, and not budge outside until we say so. Clear?'

The affirmative reply was given in a whisper, and Bony went outside and nonchalantly kicked dust over the tracks left there by Tony and Esther Harmon.

He was astride the gelding and riding out of the compound when Bert Ellis called a goodday-ee. Men at the garage stopped to watch the horse, and to them he nodded, his mind occupied with the relationship of Esther Harmon with an item of human flotsam registered as Antony Carr. Although Daybreak could be thought the last place Tony would head for, here he was, and there was the policeman's sister succouring him, and claiming there was no other than she to whom he could appeal.

Bony was riding past the Manse when Harmon appeared at the gate and held up a hand to stop him, and on Bony dismounting suggested they sit on the tree bench for 'a quiet yabber'. They sat, and the horse stood quietly in the shadow with them.

'Been asked by Headquarters for a conduct report on Tony Carr since he came to Daybreak,' Harmon said. 'What d'you know about that? And Inspector Mann being good and satisfied with what we got on Tony, too. They must think a feller's got nothing to do.'

'You been talking to the minister about it?' questioned the yardman.

'Had to. He's got to support the report, if you get me. And, Nat, there isn't anything against Tony up to the time we found the evidence in his hut and on the roof. I reckon Mann thinks the bloke defending Carr at his trial will make a hell of a lot out of good conduct since coming to Daybreak.'

'What good will that do?' the yardman asked.

'Could do a heck of a lot, Nat. You know, when we add it all up, all we got is tracks and plaster casts, and statements concerning all them casts and tracking. Enough for you and me to get fifty murderers hung. What's the motive? We say the motive lies deep in the unsound mind of a killer who has already given proof of violence before he ever came to Daybreak. We can say there is no other motive for three murders, not one matching the other two. Only in one, the Lorelli case, can we prove that Carr was at the homestead at the approximate time of that murder. Good enough for us, Nat, but I'm thinking Mann feels it isn't enough.'

'Could be the Inspector wants to make it a hundred per cent,' offered Bony.

'He'd want to do that all right,' agreed Harmon. 'I'm beginning to see it's not the lack of evidence we have, but the quality of it. Putting tracks over a jury as evidence is a different proposition to putting over fingerprints. Now if we had Tony's fingerprints on the door handle you had sense enough to preserve, we would have had something. The doctor is ready to swear that the man who strangled Kat has hands the size of Carr's, but he can't swear they were Tony's hands.

'So what have we? I'm beginning to see myself on the witness-stand, and the defending counsel saying down his nose: "What is your experience of tracking, Constable? Why were not the abos brought to the scene of the crime before eleven that morning, Constable? Where are these famous abo trackers you have been telling us about, Constable?" '

Bony burst into laughter, such was Harmon's extraordinary mimicry of a supercilious counsel.

'Funny and not so funny, Nat,' Harmon chuckled. 'Those bastards down in Perth can turn a man inside out. Anyway, jokes aside, we have time to hunt up more evidence, and I'd be obliged if you kept that in mind.'

'All right, I will,' consented the yardman. 'I suppose Tony

will be in Kalgoorlie by now, probably down in Perth.'

'About it, Nat. What they learn in reformatories! You can lock your car and keep the keys in your pocket, and he can get it going in three seconds. You can put the cuffs on him and he slips out of them just when he wants. You can badger him for hours, like I did going down to Laverton, and he don't open his mouth, not once, not even to curse me. But there's this to it, Nat: the longer he keeps in smoke, the longer we'll have to get additional evidence. So if he's free for a month, that'll suit our book. But that don't mean lying down on the job, Nat.'

'I'll keep it in mind, Mr Harmon,' said the yardman.

'You do. Riding out, I see. Call in on the abos and tell young Abie I want him up at the station'.

'I'll do that.'

'Good. We get along, Nat.'

The policeman, watching his horse loping away down the track, thrilled at the sight of him, and envied the seat of the rider. He wished he had Nat's supreme confidence; and then the reaction of the Reverend MacBride to the report he had to make clouded the picture, and sent him glowering to his office.

Bony sought the answers to questions which would assuredly have puzzled Constable Harmon, who knew nothing of the man who had forgotten to limp. Harmon had given a valuable card, and if the value hadn't been recognized at the time, it was recognized for what it was when most needed.

That Iriti and his men had held a poker hand all their own, he was sure. There was much behind the reluctance of the trackers, giving only bare essentials in their reports to their white superiors. Those trackers brought from the south would know the minds of Iriti and his fellows, so there was no actual independence of opinion between them and the local tribe.

Had Harmon known how keenly the hotel yardman sought for additional evidence to support that which he already had, he might not at this moment have been so worried. Bony hoped that Tony wouldn't be discovered, for this would indeed upset the policeman's equilibrium.

The Range flowed by on one side and the mulga forest down

on the distant floor of the world slowly revolved like a wheel, as the gelding swept down the track until he was reined to the right, to reach the aborigines' camp. There, no blue fire-smoke rose from among the great boulders. What did rise at Bony's coming was a storm of black snowflakes.

The camp was deserted.

CHAPTER 18

Trade in Blackmail

The crows had placed their seal on the camp floor and had fossicked among the ashes of the smaller fires, proving that the aborigines had departed early this same day. Still earlier a horseman had visited the camp, and had conducted his mission without dismounting. He had come from Daybreak and had left in the direction of Dryblowers Flat. Bony recognized the animal's tracks as being those of one of his horses, now supposedly running loose on the town common.

The 'mouse' was beginning to venture a fraction from his hole. His mission had been to warn or to order the aborigines to vacate a camp to which they had come only a few days before.

The trail of the exodus was easy to follow, and Bony was able to keep his horse to it at a hand gallop. Down the slope to the dry water-gutters, over them, and across the grass flats to the scrub patches, over the iron-hard red claypans, and round about the steep-sided salmon-pink sand dunes. At three miles from the damp, Bony reined back the horse and sat for a minute regarding Bulow's Range, and the dark stick which was the poppet head at Sam's Find. The township was beyond the summit. Nothing moved in all this expanse save a black dot or two puffed upward from the deserted camp of the aborigines ... the omnipresent crows.

Half an hour later, the grey was willing enough to pause a

while beneath a line of desert box trees along the shores of an ancient lake, and here Bony made a cigarette and surveyed the place where the aborigines had rested and left evidence of their recent visit to white civilization in burned matchsticks, the ends of self-rolled cigarettes, and mutton-chop bones.

There was, of course, no water in the lake. Its level surface was covered shallowly with salt, a sheet marred nowhere save by the feet of the nomads, which, beginning in separate trails, had merged into a black trail extending to the distant shore.

Bisected by the black mark, the ancient lake was now a pure white disc, edged with the deep green of trees, the pink of sand, and the grey-blue masses of spinifex. The cloudless sky above was black, the sun as near pure gold as anything not gold could be. Animation was lacking, the complete absence of motion associated with a picture which might have been painted before Time was born.

The horse making no sound, Bony felt the magic of having stepped into this picture, became a painted figure in its composition that had never moved, and never would. He was one with the stiff tussock grass about his feet, one with the gnarled and almost leafless trees about him, and artist's creation painted to give balance and perspective on the flat surface of canvas.

It was now late April, and the beginning of a period in the autumn when, in this western section of the Interior, the air is still. The summer heat has passed, and the willy-willies no longer dance over the landscape, arid and brittle. The few birds appeared to have embarked on a far journey, and even the flies and the ants must be resting.

Bony felt himself caught and held in this eternally motionless scene, until sudden revolt spun him about to gain relief by sight of the horse and its flailing tail. He sighed gustily, the sound being music in his ears. He called to the horse, to prove he had ears with which to hear.

He decided to ride around this salt lake for reasons other than the probability that near its centre the surface was too soft to bear the animal's weight. The gelding's anxiety to show off being now reduced, it was almost an hour later when they came to the place where the aborigines had stepped from the lake, continuing to travel to the northwest, and deeper into the desert.

Bonaparte was not liking this job, for he was opposed to aborigines less influenced by white law than are those in close contact with a mission station. These people were much farther beyond the mirage of civilization than those in the centre of the Continent, through which runs a railway, a string of townships, a military road, and the telegraph. He would have to deal with these people without sign of overbearing authority, and never with the threat of it.

So confident were they in their own domain that he sighted the smoke of their camp-fires rising with no twist to their columns from gums lining a dry creek, in the bed of which would be soak water. He dismounted when a quarter-mile from the camp, securely tethered the horse to an acacia, and walked on until a hundred yards from the creek, when he shouted and sat on his heels. It had been no mean achievement to draw thus close to the camp without being seen, for his presence would certainly be astonishing.

Dark figures emerged from the background of grey tree-trunks, remained a moment, faded into the background of frozen silence. Crouched on his heels, Bony rolled a cigarette and waited. Under any circumstances whatsoever, those who wait with patience live longer in this country than those who hasten.

The visitor having so rung the bell, the householder puts on his best demeanour and peers through the keyhole to see who calls. Observing that the stranger is unarmed and appears to be of friendly disposition, he sends forth one of his servants to look-see the visitor at close quarters and inquire his business. Thus, there approached Bony a youth who had undergone only early initiation, and able to understand English enough to assist with the sign language. He regarded the visitor with open curiosity, listened to the request to talk with Iriti, and retired to report. He returned minutes later, and escorted Bony to the main campfire, before which sat Iriti, Medicine Man Nittajuri, and five other elderly men. They were seated in a semi-circle, and the caller was invited to sit facing them.

About each of these seven men was the passivity of this

almost limitless land. In each was that stillness which Bony had encountered when gazing at the salt lake; the stillness of a bottomless gulf, the stillness of dark water down a deep well.

How could modern man span such a gulf? Bony had tried so often and occasionally had partially succeeded, only by being human.

He rolled a cigarette with exaggerated care. A little to one side, the young man known as Abie, Harmon's tracker, was standing on the shaft of a spear tipped with a ground-pointed dinner-knife, probably discarded by a white housewife. Actually the spear was gripped by his toes, and he could have brought up the weapon into his hand and thrown it faster than Bony could have drawn a pistol, had he carried one.

He learned that he was expected to address the Council through the young man who had asked him his business, and sensed that this young man was one of those with whom Tony Carr had associated, and proved it on noting the gleam in the dark eyes when Tony's name was mentioned.

He began by saying that Melody Sam had sent him to ask why his aboriginal friends had left Bulow's Range without telling him, and so soon after returning from their last walkabout. He reminded them of Melody Sam's generosity down through the years, that Melody Sam had always welcomed them to his camp, and they had welcomed him to their camp, having sealed him into their nation, thus making him their son, their brother, and their father.

He stared at them. They were not to be stared down; nor was he. Slowly, to give the interpreter time to work, he went on:

'One day the young lubra working for the white-feller minister was out walkabout with Janet Elder. They came back through the mulga and they came to black-fellers' sacred ceremonial ground. You never told the young lubra not go into the mulga. When she and white girl came to ceremonial ground, the lubra went back a little way and walked round it. She did not walk over it. She did not see properly the Great Snake's eggs. She saw only the white stones from the great rocks. The white girl did walk over the ceremonial ground. As I tell you, the black girl did not.

'What for you all go walkabout and then send one feller back to kill young lubra outside minister's humpy? You tell me, eh? Lubra did not go over ceremonial ground. She walk all round. She did not see-look at Great Snake's eggs. For why you say she die? She broke no black-feller law. You all broke black-feller law you kill her. Why? You tell me, eh?' He waved a hand to far-away hills. 'All black-feller away over hills away over spinifex, all black-feller knows you all broke black-feller law. You all no good black-fellers. White-feller law! Pouf! Black-feller law you broke. You tell me, eh?'

Bony had the feeling, to use a colloquialism, that the execution of the lubra was the result of intrigue conducted by rivals, and that to preserve the peace the elders had decided on her removal. Something of this nature had prompted the girl's execution, for now the elders were regarding each other with deep unease, instead of watching the accuser.

However, the murder of the lubra was less the business of white law than was the murder of three white people by a white man, and Bony was determined to use the first as a lever to unearth evidence to convict the white murderer.

For a period the elders argued among themselves, and Bony made and smoked four cigarettes while waiting for them to give him their attention. He then rolled yet another cigarette, smoked it slowly, before he continued as plain expositor rather than accuser.

'White-feller he come along and say for you to be his father and his brother, and if you don't, then he tell Constable Harmon and Melody Sam you all killed young lubra. One feller kill, you all kill. You know that. If Melody Sam and Constable Harmon been told you killed lubra, they kick you all long way from Daybreak. No more tucker. No more tobacco. No more ceremonial ground. They take trucks and gather up Great Snake's eggs and blow-'em-up rock hole, and dig-'em-up all dead aborigines.

'So you so-high little black-fellers afraid this white-feller he play hell, and you agree to trade. He not tell on you; you not tell on him any time you look-see. When he killed Mrs Lorelli, you all say wasn't Tony Carr's tracks. You say same thing when white boy killed at Sam's Find.' Now Bony risked a guess. 'When Kat Loader was killed by feller in sandshoes, you follow tracks made by same white-feller make-think Tony Carr made them. You come to root he fell over, and then you see he forgot to make-think he was Tony Carr. But you don't tell Constable Harmon. You all dead frightened white-feller tell Constable Harmon you killed young lubra. What you say to that, eh?'

It had been meandering speech, but the hearers understood it through their interpreter, and the young interpreter became increasingly indignant, delighting Bony with the strong inference that the elders had engaged in an intrigue outside the knowledge of their people.

What had they to say? After the medicine-man had threatened the interpreter and dismissed him, they had a great deal to say among themselves. At first they might have been discussing the weather, their voices low and their faces calm, but quickly it was apparent that anger was born, and the fury of it would rise like a tempest. Accusations were flung about like stones at a riot. Eyes flashed and white teeth gleamed; fists clenched and toes jerked, as though aching to snatch up a spear.

Abie, who was still on guard, became a stone gargoyle, keeping his foot on the grounded spear. Bony, aware of Abie's ability to act so fast as to deceive the eye maintained his seat on his heels, and enjoyed the spectacle of this bull-ants' nest he had stirred so effectively.

Whatever he had begun was certainly drawing to a dramatic climax, the result of the schism he had introduced cleaving these old men apart from the young men who had been closely associated in friendship with Tony Carr. Now these old men were being drafted into separate yards, the one side supporting the young men, and the others which had backed the decision to liquidate the lubra.

It was like listening on the radio to a running description in a foreign language of an all-in wrestling bout. And, in the end, it was the medicine-man, who was pinned. Unprepared for Bony's visit and disclosures, he was not wearing his official regalia of gum leaves affixed to his forehead, the mantle or sacred drawing of the Devil's Hand painted on his chest and shoulders with white ash mixed with grease. Even his magic bone, drawn through the nasal septum, had been left at home.

Notwithstanding, he still possessed authority, and, as any politician in white civilization, was a practised hand at passing the buck. He went into a trance, waved his arms and showed the whites of his eyes, and saliva dripped from his mouth, until abruptly he collapsed and appeared as one dead.

Following the exhibition, there was silence among the group and about the camp. The silence was terminated by Iriti shouting an order, and from the camp several initiated men escorted one who was obviously mastered by fear, and they were followed by all the other initiated men. Standing, Iriti proceeded to smite himself with his fists, and harangue the crowd, finally pronouncing a sentence, which was acclaimed. The chief pointed to the sun, now low in the sky, and the accused man shouted defiantly, and ran.

A woman wailed long and shrilly like a banshee. The crowd retreated. The medicine-man recovered and stalked to his own camp and little fire tended by his lubra. The old men dispersed, leaving Iriti to squat again, and Bony to roll yet another cigarette. Abie and other initiated men gathered to eat and drink their fill to sustain themselves for the hunt which would start when the rim of the sun touched the earth. The hunted was a man of middle age. He stood not a chance.

CHAPTER 19

Material for Legends

For two hours Bony and Iriti had squatted either side of a small fire, until the bucks had eaten and waited for the sun's rim to touch the western horizon. The conference had produced a bargain between them, and mutual respect as the representatives of modern and ancient cultures, rather than of the white and black races of today. For neither had complete understanding been reached without earnest effort, as the young interpreter had not been called to this most confidential conference.

When the belly of the sun caressed the earth, Iriti stood and raised an arm, to point after the condemned aborigine, and with impassive mien watched his young men race away like kangaroos into the surrounding scrub: his task of upholding justice was ended. But for Bony the ultimate triumph of the cat over the mouse was still to be won. None the less, Bony was satisfied with the bargain, and sure that Iriti would carry out his part of it.

It was night when he reached the stone man end of Main Street, his mind now on the problem of Tony Carr. Passing the hotel, he could hear the voices of men in the bar-room. As he rode into the police compound, Harmon appeared in the lighted doorway of his office, and called to him:

'That you, Nat? Been worried about you.'

'Rode farther out than I intended,' explained Bony.

The policeman didn't follow him to the horse yards, where he watered and fed the horse, and, having seen Harmon through the office window again at his desk, he crossed to the quarters to have hurried words with Esther, and arrange with her to take food to the escapee while he himself engaged the policeman in talk.

For five minutes they discussed the gelding, a mere prelude to the tossing at Harmon of a few verbal grenades.

'Did you know the aborigines cleared out this morning?' opened Bony, and Harmon's hazel eyes dwindled to hard slits beneath the swiftly lowered brows. Shaking his head, he asked:

'Something must have driven 'em. You know of a reason?'

'Yes, I do. I've been out to talk with Iriti. They were told to clear out by a man in this town. Iriti and his people will return tomorrow, and I have arranged for you and me and Sam and a few other citizens to meet them in conference at midday.'

'You have!' Anger crossed the policeman's weathered face,

128

was restrained. 'You know, Nat, I've been thinking about you. You wouldn't be playing poker all by your little self, would you?'

'As a corollary, that is what I have been doing. On your telephone you could contact Inspector Mann right now to confirm that I am Detective-Inspector Napoleon Bonaparte, of Queensland, engaged on a special assignment. On the other hand, I advise waiting a while, firstly because the conversation would probably be noted by the person now on duty at the telephone exchange, and, secondly, there is an amount of work yet to be done which you and I could do in harness. Shall I go on?'

'Yes.'

'I know who committed these murders, and the motive, Harmon. But I haven't enough evidence to advise an arrest, and what I do have would not be sufficiently conclusive to place before the Crown Prosecutor. Supporting evidence can be obtained from Iriti and his medicine-man, but you can clearly see the impossibility of presenting them as witnesses in a court. When they return tomorrow, we shall have to accept their statements through a young aborigine who speaks better English than your old-time tracker. Which is why at the conference we must have Melody Sam, and the postmaster, who is a Justice of the Peace. I expect you to hold yourself in readiness.'

The large hand which had been hovering over the telephone was withdrawn, and that final note of authority completed the change from itinerant bushman to Superior, which the astounded Harmon had been watching.

'We arrested the wrong man?' he said after a struggle.

'You arrested the wrong man. I permitted you to arrest the wrong man for a reason which will be made clear.'

'The right man: who is he?'

'He will be unmasked at the conference with Iriti.'

Harmon, who had been gazing steadily at Bony, abruptly stood and paced his office, and Bony patiently awaited his next query, in order to satisfy himself of the policeman's acceptance of the situation. He knew that Harmon was now reviewing the immediate past, weighing his own responsibility, and assessing its effect on his career and, too, on his future relationship with

Melody Sam and the people of Daybreak. Returning to his chair, he had no doubt of the truth of Bony's statement.

'I've heard of you,' he said. 'I should have guessed it some time ago; would have, too, if you had been what you are now. Yesterday I couldn't have imagined you being a commissioned officer. Now I can't imagine you as a horsebreaker. Me, I've made a few mistakes in my time, but they've been genuine mistakes. I've always done my duty, and some might say a bit more than my duty. I was rocked badly when my wife was killed, and I am still rocked every time I look at my sister. All right, so what do we do now? We can't wait until tomorrow, we can't wait till after we hear what the blacks have to say, 'cos between now and then some officer might bail up young Carr, and one or other of 'em get hurt. You know how it is when a man's on the run.'

The hard blue of Wedgwood china had faded from Bony's eyes, and about his mobile mouth was now a faint smile of approval.

'I am glad for your sister's sake, and yours, that you spoke like that. You need have no concern for Tony Carr. He's safe enough. I have attended to that. He will remain where he is until tomorrow. You concentrate on who would be competent witnesses, to assist us in placing a rope round a murderer's neck. Who understands best the language of this local tribe?'

'Fred Joyce,' Harmon promptly replied.

'Who else?' pressed Bony.

'Well, young Carr could follow 'em, but he's not here. Old Melody Sam can yabber to some of them. And I know a bit to get along with Abie, which is why I had him for my tracker.'

'It's going to be difficult, Harmon. I can go into court and swear that the man who murdered, when wearing those sand-shoes to imitate young Carr's walk, is so and so. Every police officer in the State would accept that, but would a jury? Would a jury accept as evidence statements on oath by half a dozen white citizens of Daybreak covering statements made by Iriti and his crowd? I doubt it. And to put those wild fellers on the witness-stand would be like poising a pat of butter on a red-hot needle.'

'That's all we have?'

'Yes. Only the evidence of a police inspector, supported by a crowd of wild aborigines. We have no direct evidence, no fingerprints, and the motive without such evidence might not be accepted. But there is a chance, Harmon, that the murderer will convict himself, and we accept that chance because to delay action is like the wind smoothing out his tracks.'

Bony rose to study the large-scale wall map of this enormous district. Place names were few; vacant spaces large and numerous. Only adjacent to the track to Laverton were there noted the few homesteads and wells. That track was the sole way of escape from Daybreak. He said slowly:

'Tomorrow, at sun-up, Iriti and most of his people will start back for Daybreak. They should come into sight of anyone stationed at Sam's Find at about half past ten or eleven. I'll be at Sam's Find. From your compound you can see the mine, and see me. When I wave you will know that Iriti is arriving. Then you will bring Melody Sam and the postmaster to this office to await my coming. No one other than those two. Be sure of that. Tell them they are wanted on urgent business, say, about the escape of young Carr. Clear?'

'Yes. What about . . .'

'No more questions, Harmon. No talking, and no action until you see me waving from Sam's Find.'

At the hotel, the cook having gone to bed and the maids to their homes, Bony scrounged a meal in the pantry, and was in time to meet Melody Sam locking up for the night. To the inevitable question, Bony explained how he had ridden away out in the desert, and had misjudged the time.

'Misjudged the time, me foot, Nat,' roared Sam, his grey eyes twinkling. 'Sun shining all day, too. What's coming to the boil, lad?'

'You'd be surprised,' Bony evaded. 'Tomorrow is the day, I hope. If I'm absent, don't worry.'

'What about stayin' for a pitch, Nat?' Melody Sam suggested. 'I'm not feelin' like bed for a while, and there's no one here.'

They retired to the kitchen, where they sat at a table and

drank innumerable cups of tea, as Sam was not 'on the booze'. The old man reminisced, and Bony was content to listen and relax, and to be not disappointed on receiving nothing of value towards his investigation. He had come to admire this man who towered so high above his fellows, who was so much withdrawn in isolation, and yet could stand four square in any company he chose.

It was after midnight when Melody Sam went to his room, and for the remainder of the night he maintained surveillance over and about the hotel. At break of day he took Sam his early morning tea tray, and carried out his usual chores. He had hoped after breakfast to have a few words with Esther Harmon, but was prevented when he crossed to the police compound to saddle Harmon's horse.

'Been thinking I dreamt about last night,' Harmon said. 'Your plan still goes through?'

'Yes. Keep an eye on the mine. You'll see me there, and when I wave, bring Sam and the postmaster to your office. I suppose we couldn't click on a million to one chance of someone at Daybreak able to write shorthand?'

Harmon brightened, admitting he had done 'a spot of it'. Bony beamed, and Harmon's none too sure confidence in him strengthened, it being difficult to associate this agile, unassuming bushman with the shadowy personality among the top brass.

The gelding was 'rarin' to go', and Harmon was, as always, envious of Bony's slickly smooth action of rising into the saddle and settling there before the horse realized it. The horse reared, was slapped smartly with the end of the reins, and permitted to cavort all the way down Main Street, watched by Harmon at his gate, by Fred Joyce outside his shop, Sister Jenks at her door and the children being lined up to march into school.

At a hand gallop Bony rode down the slope to Dryblowers Flat to call at the House of Elder. He was pleased to hear that the old man was away with his partner dry blowing, and additionally pleased at being invited to morning tea, served by Joy Elder under the bough roof of the floorless veranda.

'Janet's out with father, Nat,' Joy announced, her large

golden eyes steady and inquiring. 'Is there any news of Tony?'

'There is and there isn't. Then again there could be and there couldn't be,' teased Bony. 'You might say that Tony's up against it, and you might say he's in love. You answer a question?'

The girl, who had been holding an enamel pannikin in one hand and a slice of cake in the other, put both on the table and stood, saying:

'Go on. Ask it.'

'Very well, I will. Do you love Tony Carr?'

For a fleeting moment anxiety was banished by the stirring power of pride, and she answered with a simple statement:

'I couldn't love him more.'

Knowing that one day he would have to relate all this adventure to Marie, his romantic wife, Bony put another question.

'Why do you love Tony so much?'

The girl frowned, and then smiled, saying:

'Yes, I know why. It's because he couldn't cut the splinter out of my foot.' Nodding understanding, Bony munched the brownie cake. 'Well, Nat, tell me about him. You know something. I know you do.'

'I can tell you this, Joy. That Tony isn't as far away as you think, and might be closer than you think.' Gazing at the shadow of the roof where it was terminated across the rough table, he went on: 'Ah! Now the sun says it's a quarter to ten, and we have work to do. D'you think you could ride behind me on the gelding?'

Again the frown, this time accompanying the nod of assent. As Melody Sam had done, as Iriti had done, and Harmon, so now did Joy Elder see this man for the first time emerge from the man they were sure they had known so well.

'I want you to go with me to Sam's Find,' he said. 'Afterwards, I want you to go into Daybreak and do something for me. And for Tony.'

'Let's go, then.'

'Let me finish my cake and tea. Even Drake finished his game of bowls.'

133

'Who's Drake?'

'A legend of the sea, as Melody Sam is a legend of the land. Two hundred years hence they'll regard Sam as a great land hero, and you, Joy, who knows! They might look back down the years to read about their Australian Maid Marion who was married to her Robin Hood.'

'I remember Robin Hood, Nat. There's a book here about him and Maid Marion and Little John and all. And there's Ned Kelly, too.'

'Illusion flies over the veranda rail,' cried Bony, pushing his chair from the table. 'Robin Hood killed robber barons, Joy. That horrible Ned Kelly murdered policemen. Come, our steed is champing on the bit.'

The Romantic leaped into the saddle and the grey swirled about like a top until calmed with soft words and gentle hands. Joy put her foot into the stirrup, and was assisted to swing up behind the saddle. She wasn't close enough to hug the rider, but she could grip the leather about his waist. The motionless air became a wind to ruffle his black hair as the horse ran in free gallop, and the girl's red-gold hair streamed behind her, as legend has it the Maid's hair floated from her.

CHAPTER 20

The Daybreak Jury

They slid to ground in the shadow of the poppet head at Sam's Find, and Bony climbed high among the ancient timbers and surveyed the surrounding country. There was no movement, no sight of travelling nomads, but far away in line with the summit of a hill, up-thrust above the horizon, there rose two broken columns of smoke.

Without doubt the columns were smoke signals, and as it was most unlikely that aborigines not of Iriti's tribe would be in that country, there was but the one assumption: Justice had been delayed but upheld, and the man responsible for the lubra's death had paid the penalty.

When again to ground, Joy Elder wanted to know the reason for the climbing.

'First things first.' Bony informed her. 'I am expecting visitors.'

The next time he climbed the poppet head he wasn't there more than a minute. 'Now Joy,' he said, on rejoining the girl, 'listen carefully to what I want you to do. Wait here until you see me waving my handkerchief and then walk as fast as you can to Main Street. Go along Main Street, and every so often you must stop and look back to see me aloft and still waving.

'When people see you gazing this way, they will also look and see me. I want everyone in town to see me, and wonder what the heck I am doing up there. Clear? Of course it is. When you arrive at the police station, take no notice of Constable Harmon, who will be busy, and go in to speak to Esther. Be sure no one overhears you telling her that a young man she knows will not have to stay much longer in the city. Clear?'

'No. What young man? What city, Perth?'

'Just tell her quietly that a young man she knows won't have to remain much longer in the city. Repeat that.'

Joy obeyed, puzzled and a little rebellious.

'I don't understand it a bit, Nat. What do you mean?'

'Esther will know. Repeat it again.' The girl did so, and Bony smiled approvingly. 'Now wait till you see me wave.'

At the top of the poppet head, Bony made himself as comfortable as possible. The smoke columns had been cut off at base and now were rising in the still air, to feed a white-topped cloud of their own creation. Far away to the north-west he could see human figures moving about in the vicinity of the sandalwoods marking Dryblowers Flat. Nearer, much nearer, he watched the minister leave the Manse, saw Sister Jenks cross the street to the post office, could see Fred Joyce working on his utility in his yard behind the shop. Two men, of whom one was Melody Sam, sat on the form outside the hotel bar, and he could not mistake the burly Constable Harmon lounging outside his kitchen door.

The minutes passed, an estimated twenty of them, and the sun reached the eleven-thirty calibration on the celestial clock, when Bony saw the dark line of human figures appearing from the abutment of a sandhill. Iriti and his people would be keeping the appointment with White-feller's Justice.

Bony waved his handkerchief.

Joy Elder waved her hand and started walking smartly towards Daybreak. Constable Harmon left his kitchen door and made for the street, walking unhurriedly. Crossing the street, he stood before the two men seated on the form. They stood, and Melody Sam accompanied Harmon to his front gate. He was arguing, and Harmon was shaking his head.

The council staff appeared from beneath a pepper tree and was sweeping débris into a heap. Sister Jenks left the post office for her house, and Melody Sam walked slowly to the police office whilst Harmon sauntered along the street to the council staff. In his yard, the butcher was running the engine of his utility, and so clear was the air that Bony could see the exhaust smoke.

Harmon was inside the post office when Joy reached Main Street, and she deliberately looked back at Bony waving his handkerchief. Someone must have been seated under the first pepper tree, for Joy said something, and the guess proved correct when a woman appeared and gazed steadily towards the mine.

So it went on according to plan. People followed the girl's action by also gazing at Bony on the poppet head. Sister Jenks called to her, and then joined the growing crowd. Harmon appeared, this time accompanied by the postmaster, and they walked back to the station office. One by one, the people of Daybreak paused in their activities to watch Bony. Even Fred Joyce was caught when he saw beyond his yard gate a woman gazing steadily towards Sam's Find. He walked to the street, said something to the passing Joy Elder, and alternately watched her and the waving Bony.

The school bell clanged and the scholars poured from the building for their midday break. Joyce, who could not but see the policeman and the postmaster approaching the station gate, moved nearer the hotel, when he could also see Melody Sam waiting outside the station office. The three men entered Harmon's office, and all the children halted their running about and joined the people in watching the waving Bony.

Joyce moved back to the yard gate beside his shop and was met by his wife, attracted by the unusual street scene. Leaving him, she spoke to another woman, and he walked quickly to his utility and drove it from the yard. He headed for Sam's Find.

All the aborigines were now in clear view, walking in a straggling line towards their camp at the great boulders on the far end of Bulow's Range. Of the hunter's smoke columns, nothing remained other than the one smoke cloud of snowy white, suspended in the otherwise virgin sky.

Bony timed his descent to ground with the arrival of Joyce in his utility.

'What's all the excitement about, Nat?' Joyce shouted. Bony rolled a cigarette with studied care, then looked up into the open face of the man standing before him.

'Don't rightly know, Fred,' drawled the hotel yardman. 'Been doing a job for Harmon. He's been expecting the abos to come back from walkabout, and he got me to shin up the poppet head and wave to him when I could see them. Think he did see me?'

'Musta, Nat. But why all the interest in the blacks? Didn't he say?'

'Only that he wanted 'em official like. Could be they hadn't any business to leave camp so soon after getting in from the scrub. I don't know.'

'Don't like it. Don't sound sense, Nat. Harmon's got Sam and the postmaster all inside his office. You been pretty thick with Harmon, haven't you?'

'I have and I haven't, Fred.' The big man stood with heavy hands clamped against his hips. There was a puzzled expression on his face, his eyes were hard, and about the corners of his wide mouth was a greyish tinge. Bony asked:

'What d'you think is going on?'

'If I knew I wouldn't be askin' you, Nat,' retorted the butcher.

He strode back to his utility, agilely jumped behind the wheel and slammed in the gears. Instead of returning to town he headed down the track to Dryblowers, and, Bony thought likely, to meet the returning aborigines. Bony crossed to the horse, and when mounted was wondering how the meeting between Fred Joyce and Iriti with his medicine-man would end, when he heard the utility returning, and he moved off the track.

Obviously, Joyce had changed his mind. The utility passed and entered Main Street, five minutes before he did. He didn't see it outside the shop nor in the yard when on his way to the station office.

The office door was open, and Bony entered to tell those waiting with Harmon that he would be with them in two minutes. Crossing the compound, he noticed Esther and Joy Elder standing outside the kitchen, and he angled to speak to them.

'Both of you will stay here. You will not interfere.'

The voice, the blue eyes, stunned them. Esther Harmon clutched Joy's arm when they saw Bony walk to the feed-shed and enter.

'It's all right, Tony,' he assured the hidden fugitive. 'I told you I would uncover the murderer, didn't I now? You're in the clear at last.'

A sudden burst of hard breathing, movement, and Tony Carr was standing clear of the bags and the oddments of junk. His eyes were suspicious, and the fingers of his powerful hands were interlocked, and indicative of fearful uncertainty.

'I am your good friend, Tony,' he was told quietly. 'I am a detective-inspector, and tell you that you are completely free of any suspicion of these Daybreak crimes. As for breaking away from Harmon, well, there will be nothing to that. We want you to help us get the truth from the aborigines, interpret for us. Will you do so?'

Tony nodded. Bony said cheerfully:

'You can call me Bony. All my friends do. Come on.'

Together they left the shed, and Bony did his best to shield the two women from Tony, and succeeded. At the office he crowded in hard by the boy. The men with Harmon stood in shocked surprise, and then Bony was given a surprise.

'Come and sit down, Tony,' Harmon invited from behind his desk. 'Been wondering when my sister would spring you. No bad feeling with me if it's OK with you.'

The boy was too astounded to move, till Bony pushed him forward, and he sat on the offered chair, still unable to make up his mind whether to fight or run. He sat glaring at the policeman, his large hands clenched. Now seated at his side, Bony said:

'Be your age, chum. You aren't on the outside any longer.'

Melody Sam began to roar and was commanded to hold his horses. He found the situation a trifle beyond him, and flopped down on his chair and chewed his moustache. Les Thurley, the postmaster, calmly waited, and watched Bony roll a cigarette. The task seemed to take a week.

'My sojourn here at Daybreak,' Bony began, gazing steadily at each in turn, 'has encouraged me to take you into my confidence. You being responsible citizens, I expect to have your willing cooperation in furthering my investigation into the series of murders which have blighted Daybreak. I am Detective Inspector Napoleon Bonaparte, of Queensland, and now on this special assignment.'

'Anything, Nat . . . er Inspector—' began Thurley, and Bony cut him short.

'Nat will do, Les. Let's keep it at Nat. Well, Sam, will you take a hand?'

'Whatever you say, Nat,' replied Sam. 'I told you once before, you're the boss.'

'Well, here it is, gentlemen. Constable Harmon and I have been worried ever since we found out that Tony Carr was very cleverly framed for the murder of Kat Loader. We relied on foot tracks, and there's no doubt, Tony, that the man who framed you walks very much like you do, has your size feet and your weight. Now you take that look off your face and listen to me. I have several important jobs for you to work your brain on, not your boots.

'Sam, you will agree that the reports made by the aborigines on those tracks about Lorelli's homestead, and the scene of the Moss murder, were not as clear and full as might be expected of them. You, Constable Harmon, will agree that the aborigines' report, plus the plaster casts you have collected, would total ample evidence to put before a jury of a thousand aborigines, but is far from ample to place before a white jury gathered together in a city. We all agree that the foot track evidence backed by the discovery of the boots in Tony's hut, with the shoes tossed to the roof, all total sufficient evidence to send Tony to trial. That was the frame.

'The murder of the aboriginal girl triggered the remaining three. I have thoroughly investigated the girl's murder, and found it was a tribal killing. I intend to close my eyes to that, for the time being, in exchange for complete cooperation from Iriti and his people on the white murders not committed by them. What happened was this.

'The girl was condemned. She refused to go walkabout with the tribe when the sentence would have been carried out, and so a buck was sent to execute her in Daybreak. How he enticed the girl to leave her room doesn't concern us. He was wearing old boots, probably found on the town rubbish dump, but luck was against him, for he was seen by one white man, who seized the opportunity to blackmail Iriti preparatory to his own crimes. In short, in return for his silence, Iriti's trackers were to make vague reports on their reading of his tracks when wearing sand-shoes. If Iriti wouldn't play it his way, he threatened to have Constable Harmon destroy their ceremonial ground and hunt them deep into desert for all time.

'Our murderer knew he was Tony's weight and foot size, and that they walked so much alike that white bush trackers would be deceived. All he had to do to complete the forgery was to copy Tony's slight limp, which he did quite well with practice. Therefore, finding himself in the position of being able to blackmail the aborigines, he put into action his long term plan. And that was to murder three people and frame Tony Carr, leaving himself still the innocent citizen of Daybreak.'

'What for?' barked Melody Sam. 'What was his aim, Nat?'

'All in good time, Sam. First things first. Yesterday our nice

140

murderer sent the aborigines off on walkabout. I went out after them and talked with Iriti, and Iriti agreed to come back with all his people and have Constable Harmon take statements from them. To gain that assistance in nailing our murderer, I have promised to shut my eyes to the lubra affair, which, when we come right down to earth, isn't any of our business.'

'Don't agree it's none of our business,' objected Harmon.

'Damn good trade, anyway, George,' argued Melody Sam. 'We give them one. They give us three. Who's the murderer, Nat?'

'He hasn't yet declared himself,' replied Bony.

'You don't know who he is, Nat?'

Bony gazed at them all, and quietly smiled.

'Yes, I know who he is. I've tracked him on Main Street.'

CHAPTER 21

Journey to the Hangman

'We are confronted by a problem,' Bony stated crisply. 'We hold a very poor poker hand. Card one: a number of plaster casts of sandshoe and boot prints. Card two: several statements made by aboriginal police trackers in the form of secondhand reports to be offered by police officers. Card three: statements we hope to obtain from Iriti and his people partly supporting card two. It would be useless to play that three-card hand because, as I've said, what a thousand aborigines and we would believe, would not be acceptable to a jury of twelve white men.

'We must not overlook a most important fact, which is that in these days a jury on a murder case almost expects to see the crime committed before it will convict. Your city man is educated to fingerprinting. We have to admit that fingerprinting is an exact science, and that footprinting is not and of itself does not convince a white man who wouldn't know the difference between a dingo track and fox track.'

'Reckon that's so,' agreed Harmon. 'And we got no cards extra to those three you put up. And what's more, our abos aren't civilized. And there's only a few of the young 'uns who can make themselves understood in English. Fat lot of use they'd all be on the witness-stand. But you have proof, Nat, that Tony didn't make those tracks we got on to the other morning?'

'I found proof of that,' admitted Bony. 'But there is no one to support me on that particular angle. So that evidence of itself couldn't stand up in court. Actually, we are left with one course of action, and that is to make the murderer admit to his crimes.'

'How? Just tell us how, Nat,' implored Melody Sam.

'By making him come right out of his hole.'

'No answer. How?'

'In the cities, Sam, the Law has its special weapons. Fingerprinting is one. Ballistics is another. Blood classification is a third. Here the Law has its special weapons of a different kind: the weapons provided by nature, very special weapons, weapons little understood in the cities and therefore unacceptable in city courts of law. Our weapons may be listed as arts, not sciences, but nevertheless if used rightly can be just as powerfully effective in achieving the conviction of a criminal.

'Our criminal isn't exceptionally clever, but he has employed one most important attribute when carrying forward his master plan: that of patience. Like most of us here, time has less influence with him than it would if he lived in a city. He has been patient enough to make his moves at the moment which favours him, and that moment isn't when the policeman's back is turned, but when he can confidently expect nature to be on his side.

'All this denies us the use of weapons provided by science, and the weapons to our hands become blunted if used to convince city people who don't understand them, don't want to understand them. Therefore, we have to use our special weapons to compel our criminal to confess to his crimes and provide the necessary evidence in support of our own, to convict him.'

'Well, what do we do, Nat?' demanded the exasperated Sam.

'We have lunch. Then we go along to talk with the aborigines. Then we sittum-down alla same poor abo and wait. Do I have your cooperation?'

'Wait for this feller to give himself up?' queried Thurley.

'Wait for him to make his move, that we can make our move, and so on, back and forth. Just like a cat and a mouse.'

'It'll be fascinatin' to watch,' supported the postmaster.

'Too right, Nat. Give your orders,' commanded Melody Sam.

'Les Thurley, kindly return to your office and relieve the switchboard operator for security. Then connect us with Lorelli.' The postmaster left, and several minutes passed before the telephone bell shrilled. 'All right, Harmon. That'll be Lorelli's homestead. Find out how many men are there.'

At the phone, the policeman said that the cattleman and two hired hands were then at lunch.

'Ask him,' requested Bony, 'to proceed at once to block the road to Laverton at a favourable place near his homestead. Suggest wire rope to reinforce the gate opposite his house. Answer no questions.'

Marvelling at his own acquiescence, Harmon complied, succeeding in gaining swift cooperation and promising an explanation later.

'So far so good,' Bony told him. 'Now take Tony to lunch. Cross to your house as though you were comradely father and son. That will make our murderer still more curious. Sam, you and I will stroll to the hotel, where you will have lunch in the dining-room and I will take over the bar.'

There were few people on the sidewalks. There were people seated on the tree benches, and others stood idly in doorways of shops and houses. Talking gaily, Bony accompanied Sam to the hotel, and after arranging with the cook to bring him a tray lunch, he entered the bar, unlocked the front entrance, and wondered if the fly-wasp that came in and gathered a victim was the same wasp that had called on that first afternoon when he had persuaded dark-eyed, vivacious

Katherine to act with him the love scene which had tricked Melody Sam up from his gelignite-protected lair.

As a good barman should be occupied, he was polishing glasses and betting ten to one that Bert Ellis, the council staff, would be his first customer, when he lost his wager on seeing Fred Joyce enter.

'Day, Fred!' he greeted cheerfully. 'What's it to be, beer?'

'A sort of show-down with you, Nat.'

Now Bony stood square with the counter and the customer. On the counter was a two-shilling piece and a well-kept Winchester rifle, the muzzle happening to be pointing towards the barman. Bony filled a beer glass, accepted the coin and dropped it into the till. Calmly he looked into the cold grey eyes regarding him, casually glanced at the rifle, finally looked back at the man.

'A show-down?' he questioned. 'What about?'

'You were up at the poppet head waving to Harmon that the abos were coming back to Daybreak,' Joyce said accusingly. 'You said Harmon wanted 'em officially. Why? You been with him since. Over at his office with Sam and Les Thurley. Well, what happened there?'

'Can't see why you're so damned interested,' returned the yardman. 'Why don't you ask Harmon? I'm only the wood-cutter and beer puller around here. What's eatin' you anyway?'

The hard grey eyes were discs of slate. Pressed hard on the counter were the man's fists. The beer was forgotten.

'I gotta right to know what's goin' on,' asserted the butcher. 'Harmon and you tracked young Carr on that last murder. You find all the evidence. Harmon arrests him. And now Harmon and Carr are close like lovin' brothers. I gotta right to be told why. Tony Carr's my responsibility. I'm his employer and all. I ...'

'No good arguing the toss with me, Fred. There's Harmon. Ask him. He's the john, not me.

'All right! All right, Nat!'

The man's left hand casually went to the rifle grip, the other took up the glass, and, maintaining the stony stare on the barman, Joyce emptied the glass, banged it on the counter and ordered a refill.

'Me and Harmon had words last night, Nat. About nothing, really. Now be a pal and tell us what's on the board over there.'

'Well, if you put it like that . . .' Bony placed the filled glass before Joyce, and began the making of a cigarette. 'You could have pumped me up to a Sputnik when I looked in the office door and saw the meeting set up. Then when Harmon tells me to go over to his shed and fetch young Tony, you can understand . . . Anyway, I did what Harmon asked, and then we were told to sit down and keep our traps shut.

'So Harmon tells us that, from information received, young Tony was framed for those murders. At least, that's what he made it sound like. He did say, sort of stern, that he was taking us out to the aborigines' camp to ask 'em a lot of questions. Didn't say what about. I asked him, and he shut me up.'

'Yair. Could be you're speaking true, Nat. I asked Les Thurley and he said the same.' The thick fingers began drumming on the counter. The slatey eyes remained directed to the barman, and the barman drew casually at his cigarette, and appeared to be momentarily interested in another fly-wasp, or the same one.

'I'll tell you something, though, that might have a bearing, Fred.' Without being instructed, Bony refilled the customer's glass, and a smaller one for himself. 'It was the day before yesterday, in the morning, when I was over with the grey. Harmon called me into the office, all smoogey-like. He said . . . yes, that was it . . . he said: "You remember, Nat when me and you were tracking young Carr that morning he murdered Kat Loader?" I said I did, but that he wasn't with me all the time because he went home for his gun and uniform trousers, and came back to pick me up. "That's right," he said, "but you remember that rock surface where Carr changed the sandshoes for ordinary boots?" I said I did, and he said: "Well, remember the root that Carr tripped over and then smoothed out his hand prints?" I said I remember that, too. So he goes on, Fred, and says: "Now, Nat, from here on you remember right good. From that root where Carr tripped, can you remember anything funny about those tracks?"

'I did what he wanted, Fred,' continued Bony. 'I thought back to that morning, and I can't remember seeing anything funny about the tracks after Tony fell over the root. I told Harmon so. I told Harmon I'd been over all those tracks later on that morning. It was before you took the plaster casts in the yard. And I asked him what was funny about them.'

Bony sipped his drink, and worked on another cigarette, and the big man was literally dancing, his fingers tattooing the linoleum-topped counter.

'Well, did he tell you what was funny about them tracks?' he shouted, really shouted.

'All right! All right! What's up with you, Fred? You got the willies or something? Better change over to whisky, if you're going to go on like that. I'm not deaf.'

With terrific effort Joyce regained control.

'Sorry, Nat. I am a bit cranky this morning. Missus been playing up. You know, too much drink and all that. Now, look, what you been saying is very interesting. I went round Carr's tracks with the aborigines, and they didn't say anything about the tracks being funny.'

'No use arguing with me, as I said a while ago, Fred. I wasn't with you and the abos that time.'

'I'm not arguing, Nat,' Joyce almost pleaded. 'Now just tell what Harmon said was funny about those tracks. No, I don't want another drink.'

'Well, I'll tell you. I think I can repeat his very words, Fred. He said "From information I've received about Carr's tracks, after he tripped over the root he didn't limp. Not for about a hundred paces he didn't limp, Nat. Now how come you didn't notice he didn't limp when he's got a natural limp?" I said what did he think I was . . . an expert aboriginal tracker? And he said: "It's a damned funny thing, Nat, that Iriti and Abie and all them others didn't see that Carr walked without a limp after he fell over the roots." And that, Fred, is what I reckon he's taking us out to the camp this afternoon for, because if he's right, then why didn't the aborigines point out to you that Carr forgot to limp when he was all chewed up after tripping?'

Joyce was now breathing heavily. He said:

'Yes, why? A man who limps don't forget to limp, does he?'

'Not that I know of, Fred. A feller limps, he limps, doesn't he?' Bony now stared hard, meeting Joyce's hardness of eye. He was being examined patiently when previously impatience had ruled the other. Joyce was waiting for the implication to dawn in the mind of this barman, the answer to his own question: 'If a feller limps, he limps, doesn't he?' And with iron control waited for the answer: If a feller forgets to limp, then his limping was put on.

'I better be going,' he said slowly. 'Must run down to Laverton, and then on to Kal. Spot of business to attend to.'

Taking up the rifle, he withdrew the bolt sufficiently to see the cartridge case in the breech, and as though without intent, held the weapon that the barman could see it too. 'Might get a 'roo or something,' he added, laying a hint of emphasis on the 'something'. Almost carelessly, he swung the rifle in an arc to point at Bony, and his grey eyes held a hungry look as though, having had death in his fingers, he wanted to have it again.

Bony turned his back, went to the rear wall bench and returned with a tray of clean glasses. This he put down on the counter and began to polish the glasses. Then, glancing at the butcher, he asked:

'Another drink, Fred? Long way to travel. Oh, you said you didn't want another. Wonder how Harmon got Tony Carr back to Daybreak so secretly. Wouldn't be surprised if it was only a yarn, you know, about Tony getting away from him near Laverton. Harmon's been on something, with his mind dwellin' on tracks he reckons look funny. I couldn't see anything funny about them.'

'Nor me, Nat. I don't see anything funny about anything.' The slate-grey eyes were calculating, powerfully probing, and Bony was beginning to feel the strain. He failed to understand why no other customer entered the bar, and why the cook did not appear with his lunch.

'Manner of speaking, Fred,' Bony said, vigorously polishing

an already well-polished glass. 'Anyway, Tony's pretty thick with Harmon this morning, and Harmon telling me to fetch him to the office ... well, it all beats me. I give up. Horse-breaking's my line. I'm sticking to it, too. Harmon can make his arrests when and how he likes after this.'

'I don't know, Nat,' Joyce drawled with ice-cold tones. 'I've a mind ...' The rifle muzzle came again to bear on Bony. The man gulped visibly. 'I'd better be going.'

Abruptly turning, he made for the door, paused there to look up and down the street before passing from Bony's view. The quietness of the day came in, to be mocked by the bar-room clock, and Bony thankfully left his glasses, passed through the counter opening, and thumped over the floor to the street door. Noisily he unhooked it from where it was fastened to the inside wall, and whistled a tune to inform the world, and possibly Fred Joyce standing just outside, that he was going off duty, and glad of it.

From the curtained front window he could see nothing of Joyce. No one was in sight. Nothing stirred in the town. A half minute slipped into limbo and the passage door was quietly opened, causing Bony to spin about. It was Melody Sam.

Across the area of the bar-room they looked steadily at each other, before Sam tiptoed dramatically through the counter opening, and so to stand with Bony. Outside somewhere a motor engine broke into roaring life.

'That will be Fred,' Bony said, and sighed. 'He's our man.'

The vehicle was coming up the street towards the hotel. They saw it pass – a utility driven by the butcher.

'The bastard's getting away,' roared Melody Sam, and Bony said, reassuringly:

'No, Sam, he's not getting away. He's beginning the journey to the hangman.'

CHAPTER 22

The Fidget

I

From the south end of Main Street they could see the dust cloud and its dark metal tip speeding towards Lorelli's homestead and far distant Laverton. Sometimes the sunlight glinted on the utility, at others a land fold hid it.

'Five miles on a rough road, say fifteen minutes,' Bony remarked, and raced across the street to the police station, where he shouted for Harmon before entering the office. At the telephone he asked for the Lorelli homestead, and the waiting postmaster put him through at once.

'Mr Lorelli . . . quickly, please,' he asked the housekeeper.

When the cattleman spoke, Harmon introduced Bony, who then took over the receiver.

'The road block, Mr Lorelli. What have you done?'

'Strung wire windlass rope between the gateposts, Inspector. My men are there now. What's up?'

'The situation is delicate,' Bony said. 'Frederick Joyce is on his way, possibly intending to travel to Laverton. He is suffering from grave mental distress. He is armed and might be dangerous. I am hoping that when he sees you and your men at the blocked gateway he will take the branch track westward to your mill and well at the edge of the mulga. If he does not, invent excuses to stop him from proceeding past your house until I arrive there. Now back to your block, please, and let me know the result.'

'Good enough, Inspector. I can see his dust on the track beyond my window. About a mile off. He's coming like hell.'

Bony heard footsteps retreating hurriedly before silence shut away the homestead. Then: 'Harmon, your car. And guns. Sam, have trucks go and bring in Iriti and all his bucks. Have them brought here to the compound. Feed them. A ration of tobacco. Keep them here. No questions now.'

Tony Carr appeared in the doorway, and Bony beckoned.

'Tony, I want you to stay here and take over this telephone. Clear?'

'Taking over the phone is. Nothing else. What—'

'No questions. Do as you're asked . . . with a smile. Ah! Yes, Mr Lorelli. Yes! He has! Good! Excellent! Yes. I anticipated he'd take that side track, but I wanted to be sure he would when he saw you on guard at the gate. Thank you very much. Yes, remain there till we come. Thanks again.'

Bony hung up, and at once was called by Les Thurley at the switchboard. His voice was desperate with curiosity.

'My plan has worked very well so far,' Bony told him. 'The man I want has left Daybreak in a panic. I cannot answer questions just now. Please stand by your board.'

Harmon came in, carrying a rifle. He opened his safe and dragged out service revolvers, and, his arms loaded, he glared wolfishly at Bony, saying:

'It's Joyce, eh? What happened?'

'Tell you on the way. Come on!'

In the car, bucking like a steer and with Daybreak blotted out behind its dust, Bony related what had taken place in the hotel bar, and outlined his successful strategy at Lorelli's homestead.

'I wanted him to bolt, and he did,' he shouted above the racket. 'I wanted him to run for the mulga, and he's doing that right now. To make sure of it, I got Lorelli to frighten him off the Laverton road. He's just a mouse, Harmon, and I wanted him to run into a hole of my own choosing.'

'Go on! Go on! I don't get it,' shouted the policeman.

'You will. I started panic in him when in the bar, and now panic has him by the throat. I know what he's thinking. I know where he's making for, and I've driven him to his ultimate destination.'

'Where's that, damn it?'

'The aborigines' ceremonial ground, Harmon. I made him believe that you know everything, have all the evidence to hang him ten times over. He's running for the only place he believes he can hold out, shoot it out with us. But the forest, man! The forest will give us the vital evidence to raise what we have to legal perfection.'

'I could beat it out of him,' snarled Harmon.

'And have yourself tossed out of the Department. Remember, we can't charge him on what we have.'

The roofs of Lorelli's homestead shone under the sky. A dark dot on the grey-brown earth grew large and larger still, to resolve into three men standing beside the pin-like pillars that were gateposts. Bony ordered Harmon to pass the road junction to talk with Lorelli and his two hands.

'As I said, he went west down to the mill,' Lorelli informed them. 'He can't go farther than the mill. No, a range of sandhills would stop him cutting back across country to reach the Laverton road. He's run himself into a dead end.'

2

Harmon stopped his car on the crest of a long and gradual descent to the motionless windmill topping the well, with the mulga forest immediately beyond. It was the type of country seemingly open, without shadows, deceptively massed termite hillocks and dry gutters to provide an army of snipers with adequate cover. And by the well stood Joyce's utility.

'Don't see him,' complained Harmon. 'Could be lying doggo behind the well-coping. You like it, you tell me, Nat. Damn! Ought to be more respectful.'

'I don't like it,' stated Bony. 'You ever been shot at?'

'Once. But then I was hot. Now I'm stone cold. Makes a difference. How are you with a rifle?'

'Better with an automatic, my own. But I left it at home in Queensland. No sign of Joyce down there. He could be in the forest; and, as you point out, he could be lying in wait behind the well, or behind the nearest forest mulgas. Only one way to settle it.' Bony glanced at his companion. 'I seldom wager with money. I bet a pound he's in the forest. Let me drive – in case I lose. You get in the back with the rifle. And if you have to shoot, wing him.'

Harmon wormed his way over the seat-back, and Bony took the wheel. Above the noise of the engine he heard the policeman checking the rifle. The forest, the motionless windmill came up to meet them, and a crow flew ahead and settled on the mill's topmost vane.

'What about that bet?' Bony asked Harmon, and Harmon said:

'Not a chance. I happened to see that crow.'

The crow proving that Joyce was neither inside his utility nor concealed behind the well-coping did not remove the possibility that he was taking cover behind one of the mulgas at the forest edge less than three hundred yards distant. The bird cried defiance at the car and flew away, and Bony eventually braked to a halt behind the utility to gain as much cover as possible from a marksman behind a tree.

'I'll prospect,' Bony said.

Exhibiting nonchalance he did not feel, he passed round the utility to look into the driving cab. There was nothing there. On the tray of the vehicle were two four-gallon drums, one containing petrol, and the other water, without which no journey in this country is undertaken.

At the mill troughs cattle had come for water and the ground hereabouts was churned by their hooves. There was, however, no difficulty in detecting that Joyce had walked from his utility to the forest. He weighed a hundred and sixty pounds, perhaps a little more. The good tracker could see the imprints of his boots; the expert now decided that Joyce had been carrying a load, adding to his weight another forty or fifty pounds.

'In the forest without doubt,' Bony said on joining Harmon behind the cover of the utility. 'Ignition key in the lock. He carried a load – food, most likely, in addition to his rifle.'

'If he's thinking of lying up and shooting it out, that won't help him any,' Harmon said. 'Time's against him.'

'So is the forest,' Bony asserted. 'And the weather.'

'The weather!' snorted the policeman. 'Do we take the utility back to Daybreak?'

'We could be charged with illegally using,' patiently Bony reiterated. 'Joyce might have gone into the forest to catch rabbits, or to compose a poem on the magic of those trees. On returning he would find his property stolen.'

'All right, Nat. Stop talking like a bloody lawyer.'

'The petrol could evaporate whilst the owner is away. Get me an adjustable wrench, and then empty that drum.'

Crawling under the vehicle, Bony unscrewed the tank plug, waited for the tank to empty, then screwed back the plug.

'Must have been ten gallons in the tank,' he said. 'How much in the drum?'

'Full,' replied Harmon.

'Fourteen gallons on leaving Daybreak, about. Food in a sack, by his tracks. Yes, Harmon, he must have loaded up when he knew we were in conference. He must have prepared his getaway before he had that little gossip with me in the bar. And so it was that little gossip over the bar counter which decided him to bolt for the forest, and not for Kalgoorlie. Now back to Daybreak.'

There was no firing from the mulgas as the car moved up the slope. Neither man spoke during the journey back to Lorelli and his road block. There, Bony asked:

'D'you think the weather will hold?'

'Now the man's talking about the weather,' snarled Harmon, and Lorelli, tall, lean, dark, gazed at the sky and nodded. Bony stooped and plucked a handful of dust from the ground, held his hand high and permitted the dust to trickle through his fingers, and watched intently the dustfall.

'Yes, the weather will hold,' he said, smiling. But there was no smile in his abruptly blazing eyes.

3

It was three o'clock.

The aborigines, numbering close on forty males, from old men to stalwart youths, had eaten from the larders of Daybreak, and now were smoking or chewing tobacco given by Melody Sam, who had also seen to it that their dilly-bags were filled with spare plugs. Outside the compound, the white

153

population, including the children who had refused school, were gathered in a wildly speculative crowd.

Bony had had ten difficult minutes with Mrs Joyce, finally being satisfied that she knew nothing of her husband's murderous activities. And now he took Harmon and Melody Sam aside from the aborigines, Sam having been brought up to date with the latest development. With cold voice and icy eyes, Bony said:

'Sam, all these white people out there are yours. They are under your command. All these aborigines here are in my command. Harmon, now is your chance. You are the Law. You are to keep a record of everything that happens, dates and times. I shall get this fellow without losing a man, and hand him to you on a golden salver garnished with positive proof of his guilt. Where's Tony?'

Sam bellowed for Tony, and the young man hurried from the office.

'Tony, you have never been in the army, where you would have learned much,' Bony began. 'No discipline has been your downfall. You shall be my aide. Responsibility will be beneficial, and you shall be loaded with it. You will stay by me, and carry out any order I give. I don't want to turn round and find you picking buttercups in the next State? Clear? Now we will confer with Iriti and his medicine man.'

Melody Sam's eyes were shining with excitement. Tony's shoulders had lost their slouch and his mouth was grimly firm. Harmon looked resigned. He might be the Law, but felt that something had slipped somewhere. Bony did not call Iriti; he went to him.

The scene was not so strange as might appear. With the edge of his hand Bony smoothed the ground, and with a finger rapidly drew a map of the mulga forest, Lorelli's well and the utility, Daybreak and Dryblower's Flat, and especially marking the aborigines' ceremonial ground. About this sand map, white men and black elders squatted on heels, the others standing behind them. When Bony spoke, the young man who had interpreted at the first talk now assisted.

'Fred Joyce run away in his utility. He has a rifle and

ammunition, and plenty of tucker. He left the utility at this well, and carried his rifle and tucker into the mulga.

'Why did he do that? I tell you. When he left Daybreak he thought Constable Harmon was going to arrest him. He travel pretty quick. When he left Daybreak he said to himself: "No good going to Kalgoorlie because Constable Harmon he send mulga wire to police fellers there to arrest him. No good going anywhere to get away from Constable Harmon. Better to make for ceremonial grounds." There he'll be safe from black-fellers, knowing they can't kill him on their ceremonial ground, and would not risk one of themselves being killed there. He knows that if white men go for him there, he can shoot one, perhaps two or three before they kill him. Then there will be blood on the sacred place.'

Bony's finger lifted from the spot on the sand map. He waited for what he had said to sink into minds having to span a gulf to reach his own. They grunted softly, and he knew they could see the picture. They were now not mentally withdrawn. They waited with restrained eagerness to be shown the next picture.

'Big-feller policeman down in Kalgoorlie, he tell Constable Harmon to bring Fred Joyce down to Kalgoorlie, where old-man white-fellers say what they do with him. Us no killum Fred Joyce, no bash-um, nothing like that. We tell Fred Joyce to come out of mulga, and he say "No fear." He say: "You come here for me, I shoot." Okee?'

This picture they understood.

Now Bony stood up with both hands filled with dust. They watched the dust fall in thin streams to the ground, and not a breath of moving air motivated it. They watched him look steadily at the sky, and then at the scanty foliage of the ancient gum tree. They were beginning to understand this new picture. Down on his heels again, Bony said:

'You fellers tell Fred Joyce come out of mulga. You go on telling, eh? Sun go out, and come up, and go out again, and up again, and you all the time tell Fred Joyce to come out from the mulga. Tell him mulga no good feller. Tell him Constable Harmon he good feller. What you say to that?'

Iriti spoke to his medicine-man. Nittajuri stood with dust in his hands and watched it fall. He went away to the gum tree and appeared to be looking for insects beneath its shredding bark. The sunlight gleamed on his dark chocolate skin, as on patches of satin. Beneath the tree he took up dust and let it fall.

On returning to the group, he talked with Iriti, and presently Iriti agreed with the decision he made. The chief took time, probably to impress his people, before saying in effect:

'Fred Joyce we turn into a mulga seed, all nice and tight inside the case. We burn and burn, and the case cracks open and the seed jumps right out into Constable Harmon's jail.'

CHAPTER 23

The Cat

The first and second nights since Frederick Joyce fled into the forest of broad-leaf mulga passed without incident. The stars had gleamed without winking. The weather continued utterly calm. By day, the occasional twitter of love birds and the cawing of crows did not penetrate into the forest, nor did the voices of the men who had been stationed in a broad-water gutter giving protection from a rifleman lurking behind the mulgas.

The camp site had been chosen by Iriti. It was a mere two hundred yards from the forest on the rising slope to Daybreak. Why it was chosen Bony didn't bother to ask, for, like the cat, he was completely relaxed and confident that the end would come with the emergence of the mouse . . . if the weather remained static.

Iriti and his elders adopted Bony's plan with the enthusiasm with which they would have agreed on a long and endurance-testing manhunt. This was a new experience, this employment of their 'magic' opposed to a white-feller killer wanted by the white-feller policeman, and, like all primitives, they determined to be triumphant.

Immediately following agreement to cooperate, Iriti had sent his young men and women to patrol the entire circumference of the forest, with orders not to be seen by the fugitive, and to send up a smoke signal did he decide to leave it.

In camp with Bony were Harmon and Tony Carr. Melody Sam and Ellis with another man visited them at night and brought food and water. Iriti and Nittajuri and two very old aborigines rostered themselves to attend a small fire fed by no more and no less than five sticks placed like the spokes of a wheel, the fire of glowing coals being the hub. In turn each man crouched over this tiny fire for an hour, and at the end of his period of duty the man would stand, rub the cramp from his legs and wipe perspiration from his face.

They were not bored. Constable Harmon was. He said:

'If this thing works, Nat, I'll hop on one leg from here to Laverton.'

'Don't be rash,' advised Bony. 'You would look damn silly.'

'I've known a number of instances of magic that can't be explained,' Harmon went on. 'But I've never heard of pulling a man out of a belt of scrub like pulling a cork out of a bottle. Their thought transference, or telepathy, might act on another abo, but Fred Joyce is a white man.'

'But just as susceptible to the nature weapon we are now using,' countered Bony. 'Apart from the aborigines' magic, which we may or may not believe in, we must admit to the power of our nature weapon. Which, Harmon, is a state where sound is absent. You have encountered this phenomenon for a moment or two, an hour or so. I have, too. An entire night when not one tiniest sound reaches the human ear. You mentioned an occasion when on patrol you felt compelled to wake your sleeping camels that their neck bells could clang. In the forest there is now that kind of silence.

'Men have endured long periods of solitary confinement. Still, in the dungeon there is not the absence of sound, no matter how silent it may appear to be. The prisoner himself creates sound of movement, of his own respiration, of his own voice, and these vibrations rebound from the walls for his ears to register and his mind to feed on.

'But out here, in the forest, there are no walls, and what sounds the prisoner himself makes are engulfed, never to return to comfort him. If there be no natural sounds to come to him, he is subjected to an unnatural imbalance.'

'All right; then why the mumbo-jumbo over that little fire?' persisted Harmon. 'It's not the fire that makes 'em sweat after an hour of looking at it.'

'When in association with these really wild aborigines,' Bony continued seriously, 'you must have met with many puzzling incidents. There is, for you and me, and other bushmen, only the one explanation – the power of thought projection, or telepathy. Put this to an anthropologist, and he smiles, retreats to his academic castle and lowers the drawbridge.

'It doesn't matter at the moment whether you or Tony agree with me or not. It is my belief that those aborigines have been continuously strengthening our nature weapon – minus sound – by willing Joyce to come to us. No matter if we do agree it is a steam-hammer to crack an egg. In addition, the aborigines are giving valuable assistance to achieve the same end. They are watching every yard of the forest's edge and, without being seen by Joyce, will make him sense they are there. If we liken the weapon of silence to a knife, we may say they are keeping a razor sharp blade beautifully polished. They will, I think, give you a surprise before long.'

'Hope so,' grumbled the still doubtful policeman. 'There they go again. The medicine man's going to give the telepathy stunt a go.'

Later this day Harmon received his surprise. From the air, so it appeared, materialized the one time police tracker, Abie. He advanced and proffered to the policeman a .44 Winchester repeating rifle. Harmon frowned, and Tony Carr gazed from it to him, saying:

'That's the boss's rifle. He's only got that one. He's lent it to me now and then.'

'I suggested to Iriti that the rifle might be taken from Joyce without violence,' Bony explained. 'We shall now be able to move about without the risk of being shot at.'

'They're good, Nat, we got to admit,' Harmon said delightedly. He slapped Abie heartily on the back, and Abie grinned his pride and pleasure. He wanted to know how it had been done, and had Abie speared Joyce to do it. Abie shook his head, and stalked away. And vanished.

Now they could stand and, standing, could look at the forest.

'I've seen them trees a million times,' Tony said, 'but I've never seen 'em like that. I don't want to see them either. Drive any man crazy.'

The day passed, and the unwinking stars were again glued to the celestial bowl. Sam and his assistants came with food and water, and Sam chuckled gleefully when told about the rifle.

'Must have come on the boss when he was asleep,' Tony contributed, and Melody Sam playfully dug his fist into Tony's ribs.

'He wasn't asleep, lad. If he'd been asleep he'd have had the gun cuddled up under him like a bitch cuddles a pup. Look at them there sitting round the fire, working like hell on Fred. They can't do a thing without putting on an act. Got to kid themselves.'

'Mumbo-jumbo!' snorted Harmon. 'They can do enough without that fire-squat act.'

They sat about a little fire of their own, and presently Sam suggested for the tenth time that Bony tell them what lay behind the murders at Daybreak.

'It would be indiscreet to do so before the arrest of Joyce,' Bony said, 'but it is a man's prerogative to be indiscreet now and then. So I shall give you the bones of this case, which could well be included in your volume of *A Thousand Homicides*.

'When I decided to come to Daybreak in the guise of a horse-breaker, I loaded myself with many disadvantages, and one of them was being a nomadic stranger in a small and very tight community, where everyone almost is related to everyone else.

I couldn't ask a hundred careless questions and hope for even one of the answers to be productive. I could trust no one with the exception of Sister Jenks. So I had to wait for the ace to come my way, the top card giving me the motive for those murders.

'You came up with the ace, Harmon, and I did not then recognize it for a card, let alone an ace. We were taking tea with your sister, and somehow the subject of Kat's interest in me came into the conversation, and you mentioned that the Loader women always knew what they wanted, and referred to Fred Joyce as being in the position of supporting you. Thus you informed me, indirectly, that Mrs Joyce was Sam's grand-daughter, and Kat's sister. That card became the ace only after Kat was killed, and the entire plan behind the murders was then made plain.

'At some time in the past you, Sam, fell out with Mrs Joyce, and you concentrated your affection on Kat, and made her your heiress. Kat was the bar between Fred Joyce and your money. In short, the idea was to remove the bar by progressive steps, and at the same time build up an unbreakable frame about a young man whose reputation before coming to Daybreak was bad. He, therefore, championed the young man all the way through, so that, when his final step had been taken, he'd be the last person to be considered in such a role. To champion the underdog and frame him for the murders brought him right against Melody Sam and all his property. Not the first time in criminal history that a man has committed several murders to reach the one person standing in his way, thus evading sus-picion.

'Joyce foresaw that, following the removal of Katherine Loader, her grandfather would be compelled to turn to his other granddaughter. Katherine was to be the last murder, and the series would be cleared up with the hanging of Tony Carr.

'The murder of the lubra gave him what he thought was an excellent start. That killing was tribal business. By chance he happened to see it done, and he blackmailed Iriti, who was to pay by imposing bad eyesight on the trackers when called to assist the police on the murders of Mrs Lorelli and Moss, and thus preserve his building of the frame against Tony Carr.

'He was approximately Carr's weight and foot size, and practice enabled him to copy Tony's limp. The price of black-mail was: one, to make no positive report on who wore the sandshoes when Mrs Lorelli and the boy were killed, although normally the trackers would know it wasn't Tony, and that it was a person imitating his walk; and, two, they were to state definitely, when they tracked after the killing of Kat Loader, that it was Tony Carr.

'All beautifully tidy if, when on his last murder, Joyce hadn't tripped, and in anger forgot to limp. I am sure, Tony, you would never forget to limp, because you cannot stop limp-ing.'

'The rotten, dirty, blackhearted—'

'Now, Sam, that'll do,' Bony chided, and stopped him like shutting off a siren. 'I am convinced that Mrs Joyce has no knowledge of all I have outlined. Now you will understand how this is a classic case of the police knowing without the shadow of doubt who committed a dastardly crime, and not possessing evidence clear enough to gain a conviction.'

'As yet,' snarled Tony Carr. 'He done right by me. He give me things. He was decent to me when other people bashed me down. And all the time he was going to do that to me. You're all the same – all rotten stinkers. A feller can't trust no one.'

Quietly Bony said: 'There is one person, Tony, you can trust right now, and without any doubts, and you know who she is.'

Tony rose and strode off into the darkness, and the men sat on and thoughtfully smoked. Eventually Sam said:

'He'll come good. I'll look after him.'

Sam and his assistants were halfway up the slope to Day-break when they were halted. They turned towards the in-visible forest and strained their ears. In the camp Harmon and Bony also directed their eyes to the invisible forest. From it, from the very heart of it, a voice came to them, screaming defiance; so small a voice, so lonely, that it might have come falling down through space from one of the unwinking stars.

The man squatting over the little ceremonial fire lifted his head, and turned his face to Bony and the policeman. The white teeth gleamed as the mouth smiled with triumph.

CHAPTER 24

The Mouse

I

The man who trudged over the light-red sand deposited on the firm earth, and on which the mulgas stood like toy trees, was hotly angry. That damned barman! He had always felt there was something wrong with his front. He was too easy, too la-di-da, and too thick with Harmon from the very day he came from out of the bush.

He should have shot him cold when he had him at the end of his rifle, instead of being tricked into thinking he was a half-abo dope.

It was no good kicking himself to death, not now. He had a job ahead which would need clear thinking. He was in a bad jam, but no jam was ever so bad a feller couldn't force his way out. There he would be safe enough from Harmon and that blasted barman, if he took a hand in the game, and as for the abos, well, even if they came into it, which wasn't likely, they wouldn't run the risk of a killing, not on their ceremonial grounds. Anyway, if it came to the worst, and it might, he'd do a lot more killing before they got him.

Once he stopped to lower the sack of food to the ground and wipe his face. He glanced back, and could see his footprints winding in and out of the green-brown trunks to merge finally into this plastic forest. Leaving those tracks couldn't be helped. He wasn't Tarzan to swing himself from tree to tree, and there was no other way to avoid leaving his trail. There were no areas of broken surface rock over which he could skip and jump, not like that country away to the north where he could trick even the abos.

Hoisting the sack to a shoulder, and with the rifle slung over the other, he pressed on. Tracks! Where the hell had he gone off the rails that night he killed Kat? Yes, that was what the barman said Harmon had said. He remembered tripping over that blasted root, and Harmon had said that Tony Carr had forgotten to limp, or that he had forgotten to limp like Tony Carr.

That was a snag all right, forgetting to limp after all the practising he'd done, so that he'd come to limp like Carr without thinking to do it. Well, so what! The blacks couldn't have told Harmon. Who else? Only that barman chap. Creepy kind of bird. Never seemed to notice a bloke exceptin' sometimes, and then his eyes were steady and kind of calculating. But the blacks must be behind Harmon. He'd sent for them, and Nat had been told to climb the poppet head to signal when they came. And they had had young Tony planted in the shed behind the compound. Nothing made sense, and yet, by hell, it did.

Anyhow, it could wait. He could see the stones of the ceremonial ground between the set up of trees, and the open space widened at his approach and there was the heap of rocks that would be a fortress he could defend to the last kick.

The accompanying dark cloud lifted when he left the trees and sunlight became strong, or so it seemed. He kicked a marker stone savagely out of his way, walked through the stone-marked passage to the head of the design, and so reached the rocks and ended his flight. It was good to be surrounded by them, to remove the weight of the tucker he had brought. And plenty of cold, clear water in the rock hole.

Frederick Joyce settled into his fortress. There was a handy place where he could lie comfortable, and command every yard of this open space.

Here he was one up on the aborigines, anyway. Somewhere close was their treasure house where they kept their pointing bones, and their rainstones their father and mother churinga stones. And there were the dead ones all around, too, and they'd all stand up and go to market if one drop of blood was spilled on this place. The abos wouldn't try for him, not here they wouldn't. Harmon and the others might, and then the abos might start something with them.

2

Nothing moved; not a leaf of the distant trees, not a bird. There were no rabbits, no jerboa rats, no banded ant-eaters. The only tracks he had seen of anything living were those he himself had made. It was a great forest, anyone would have to admit. He had seen grass growing, following a good rain. But it hadn't rained since early last spring. Must have been August; eight months back, and the ground here must be extra porous, because even after the rain and the grass sprouted, it didn't last long.

No wind to blow it away if there was grass. Quiet spell. Often happened at this time of year. Quiet was right. Joyce listened, and could detect no sound. It was so quiet that if the sun crackled he could have heard it.

When night came the soundlessness was emphasized by the elimination of sight. The mind, occupied by day with what it registers through the eyes, by night seeks to register objects by sounds, and under normal circumstances succeeds.

At first Joyce was confident that he would hear the approach of humans in this sound void. He became so sure of this that throughout this first night he slept, if fitfully, and when day broke, ate a breakfast of cold beef and bread.

Again he surveyed the scene, which was not even fractionally altered from the previous day. Nothing moved in the motionless air save the smoke from his cigarette. He heard nothing save when he sniffed or breathed heavily, and as Bony had experienced when gazing over the salt lake, so did Joyce come to be impressed by what he saw, as a picture without perspective, a flat surface.

The rising sun gave warmth which he didn't need. He cleaned the rifle, which required no such attention. He counted his stock of cartridges, and if he hit the bull's eye every time, he would achieve two hundred and three dead men. Then he fell to tossing rock chips to strike against a boulder, and found the sound pleasing. As hour followed hour and still nothing moved, he began to doubt that Harmon or the aborigines were taking any interest in him. This puzzled him, then dismayed him, eventually angered him. He was all set to make a last stand, and no one would act the scene with him.

It was not until the afternoon that the tension waned and reaction found him mentally exhausted to the point that he slept without warning. On waking he was mentally calm, and after a swift survey of the surroundings, he ate, and drew water from the rock hole with the aborigines' tin bucket.

There had been no attack, and still no sign of it. Harmon hadn't dared to try it on in broad daylight, and the blacks most likely had gone on strike. The night could be different, and night wasn't far off. At long last the sun set, and, the shadows having departed with it, there remained the countless identical trees standing on the ground of salmon-pink sand, which in the gloaming appeared to shine in rivalry with the evening sky. Then the trees drew away and the white stone of the ceremonial ground whitened still more and looked just like the sand-polished skulls of the aborigines supposed to be buried hereabout. These sank from sight, and only the darkening sky was left – a circular plane of stars cold and remote.

The objects he could no longer see became magnified and took to themselves personality. They were at first benign. Then they were contemptuous. He could not hear them, but they were discussing him. Yet, it wasn't the trees whispering about him; it was Harmon and that yardman and Iriti and his bucks. If only he could hear something. The silence, which at first was a friend to betray the approach of an enemy, became his enemy – a Thing which made his ears ache from the strain of listening.

Seated there among his rocks, gripping the rifle-stock so hard that cramp seized his hands, Joyce existed through the hours of his second night. He wanted daylight, and when light did come, all the furniture was in its place, and he didn't think to look for 'the cat'.

Throughout the morning nothing happened. Nothing moved. And such was the strain he placed on his eyes, he thought not of watching the ants. Not a sound came to him from the encircling forest. His ears were aching intolerably, and to relieve them he beat lightly on the aborigines' water tin, lightly, that Harmon and his men wouldn't hear it before he saw them.

Some time in the afternoon he decided he could not remain inactive any longer. They wouldn't come for him, so he would go hunting for them. He'd shoot the first bastard he sighted. One part of his mind urged action, the other frantically pointed out the stupidity of leaving his fortress; the first being dominant and soundly berating the second for its cowardice. He heard the argument in progress, and realized he was talking loudly. He listened to his own voice, and could hear the sounds comprising the utterance speeding from him like little bullets, and knew they would never return.

Nothing did in this blasted forest. He snatched up his rifle and raced to the trees.

He was the only living thing in a picture of trees, and presently he walked right through it to be one with another picture of a great open space; the ground gently rising to the line of Bulow's Range broken by Daybreak and Sam's Find. In this picture also were the ghost gums where Bony had found Tony Carr mustering courage to cut a stick from a girl's foot.

He stood against a mulga trunk and made a cigarette, the tough bark pressed comfortingly against his broad back, the rifle leaning against the tree at his side. He struck a match, and the sound was good to hear. The flame was almost invisible in the strong sunlight, and the pale smoke rose before his face. The picture came back to him, and he frowned, for there seemed to be something out of place in it. He stared at it, up and down and from side to side and into the four corners. There was something. Ah! against the white trunk of one of the ghost gums there was movement. Damn it, there was an abo behind that tree, not more than a hundred yards distant.

Maintaining his gaze on the white trunk, his hand went down to his side for the rifle. The hand groped for it, found only trunk as rough as a wood rasp. He had to remove his gaze from the distant ghost gum to locate the weapon. And did not see it.

3

The shock had been severe, and now, as he crouched among the rocks at the ceremonial ground, his world was filled with sound . . . the noise of his erratic breathing. Those blasted abos had got his rifle, took it as he was standing with his back to the tree; took it when the rifle was leaning against the tree trunk, within six inches of his thigh. They had waited for him to do that, to use both hands making a cigarette, and then one had caught his attention by moving out a fraction from the ghost gum, and another had been right behind the mulga waiting to lift the gun.

There were the tracks going away to the next mulga, a clear set of naked feet. He had chased the thief to the next tree, and the next, and had to give it away and run like hell back to the rocks. And now he had no gun, nothing to keep the black scum off. Well, he wasn't done yet. He'd shift into that rocky doorway and have a heap of stones ready for them, and he fell to gathering this makeshift ammunition with frantic energy.

Afterwards the hours passed, and there was nothing to see and nothing to hear. The sun slid down and the evening came, and with the certainty of coming darkness came the terror. It would be completely silent again, and he would hear anyone approaching . . . but no, it had been dead silent when he leaned against the mulga, and he hadn't heard the abo creep up behind it and take the rifle. What use was the silence? They could be just round the rock corner and he wouldn't hear them. They could be right in his hair and he wouldn't know until they tugged it out. They could be breathing down his neck and he wouldn't see them.

Seated there with his back against rock and his flanks guarded by rock, Joyce imagined the stars above being blotted out by a dark figure making ready to drop a great slab of rock upon him. He imagined black hands reaching for him from the blackness which he faced, and terror increased to spur his tortured ears to give warning of death, which was magnified a thousand fold by a mind now embattled with the threat of disintegration.

He might have found solace in the crackling wood had he dared to make a fire. He might have found a balm to his ears had he beaten the blacks' water-bucket with a sliver of rock. He suffered no remorse; did not recall the gurgling sounds emitted by two women, not the guggling of a blood-drowning young man. Nothing so melodramatic as that. How could remorse, memory, influence these hours of impenetrable darkness in which invisible hands might be clamped about his own throat, and he would listen to his own death-rattles?

Strange, and yet perhaps not so strange, that he came to feel the proximity of black hands in the blackness about him. Perhaps not so strange when faintly he saw tiny globules of pitch surrounded by the whites of approaching eyes.

He yelled and fled from the rocks.

In the open of the ceremonial ground, where the stars shed a little light, where the air was free, where there were no confining walls, he began shouting his defiance of the creeping, sneaking, snivelling aborigines, and of that swine of a Harmon, and of that many-times-accursed barman. It all went from him, ricocheting among the stars.

The stars came down to crush him. The trees marched in to smother him. He was buried beneath the pounding of their silent feet. And when he clawed his way up from the pit, it was day.

He ran back to his rock pile. Nothing was changed. The silence was now a thing living with him, like his shadow, to follow always. His ears ached from the buffeting received from his hands, and the drums burned with pain. His face, known to all the people at Daybreak as one of open frankness, was slack of flesh and lined perpendicularly. His eyes, once so warmed with apparent humour, were without lustre, the irises of the pale malevolence of those of a shark just brought to the gaff.

4

It was the third day when he began to poke at his ears in an effort to relieve the feeling of pressure on the drums. The pressure was accompanied by a faint and persistent hissing noise, until it faded into the breathing of a black-feller behind him. The silence was now pressing upon him from all sides, and when he shouted, the sound was outside the pressing force.

He made a fire and boiled water, and the crackle of the tree débris he had gathered was like glorious music. Waiting for the tea to cool, he was seized by the childish whim of tossing on to the fire the store of cartridges. From behind a rock he shouted gleefully as the cartridges exploded, seeing himself in the centre of a battle, the last heroic stand, and shouting his defiance at the encircling trees that wouldn't move one solitary leaf to prove that they were living things, and prove to him that he was a living thing too.

On the fourth day, discarding all discretion, he fled to the northern extremity of the forest and was confronted by the steep face of the breakaway down which Bony had ridden a few weeks before. The rock wall was marked with crevices. It was surmounted by desert jamwoods and tufts of spinifex. In a rock crevice there was a thing with eyes. He could see the white about the graphite centres. There stood an old burned tree stump. It had eyes, too. They flickered, went out, appeared. They were fixed to the stump.

The 'mouse' squeaked and flicked himself back to his rocks. Now, however, the rocks withdrew the illusion of security, and the following night he spent with his back against a tree trunk.

On the morning of the fifth day he was walking to find the rocks and that rock hole where the water lay dark and deep and cool. He heard himself sobbing, and one part of his mind said he was a fool, because he wasn't sobbing. How could he hear, when he would never hear anything again? He saw the tracks of naked feet and halted to gaze stupidly at them until the lucid part of his mind understood their significance.

The tracks sent him running over virgin ground, presently to be halted again by another trail made by naked feet. He veered away and kept on running, and then it seemed that no matter which direction he took, he came to the prints of naked feet.

Out of this damn forest! He must get out of it. No more could he stand it. He was indeed out of the mulgas, stumbling over uneven ground which bore tussock grass and saltbush. Was that a crow he heard? Never, never would he shoot another crow. And there were men sitting on the ground, three of them, looking at him as he stumbled up the slope. There was George Harmon. And Iriti. And the barman was sitting in the middle.

'George!' he screamed. 'Say something! Say something!'

CHAPTER 25

Repletion

As Melody Sam was often to recall, it was a wonderful day for the Irish. Assisted by his barman-yardman, he served free drinks for an hour. The manager of his general store was instructed to entertain the children with sweets, soft drinks and fruit until the stock ran out. And Tony killed the fattest beast on hand for the aborigines to cart off to their cooking fires.

At five o'clock Melody Sam ordered everyone from his hotel. At six o'clock Bony was seated with Constable Harmon in the police office, the desk littered with documents all signed and witnessed by Justice of the Peace Les Thurley. Harmon was tired yet elated.

'Fred Joyce won't get out of this lot,' he said, waving to the litter. 'He signed all my transcribed notes of what he told us on coming out of the forest. You know, Nat, I don't think any killer so completely damned himself by giving dates and events, plus conversations and persons who can testify against him.'

170

'When these cold and calculating men break, they don't half do it,' Bony said firmly. 'They build themselves high on vanity, and once vanity evaporates, they're like an unset jelly.'

'A wonderful job, Nat.'

'We all did a good job together, including Iriti and his people.'

'Yes, Iriti did too. What about that abo murder? You doing anything about that?'

'I'll tell you the facts.' Bony rolled what might be called a cigarette, and Harmon waited patiently. 'This time last year Janet Elder and other girls were out with the aboriginal lubras, and Janet persuaded Mary to return home straight through the forest. They came to the ceremonial ground, and Mary skirted wide out from it, and Janet walked through it.

'On the following day or the day after, a black-feller named Wintarri, or something like that, was in the forest and saw the girl's tracks. He was a nasty fellow who had been secretly pursuing the reluctant Mary. There were a lot of cross trails like wrong totems and such, but the point is clear that Wintarri reported that it was Mary who had crossed the ceremonial ground, not Janet Elder, knowing that this false information would result in Mary's execution.

'He wasn't a young man. He possessed influence in the tribe. His lying statement was worth something, and there was temporary disagreement when the elders of the tribe decided to send a man to kill Mary in Daybreak. On being assured by me that it was the white girl who crossed the ground, not Mary, Iriti sent for the unsuccessful pursuer of the maiden and sentenced him to run from death. He received a little more than an hour's start. The avengers Iriti sent after him did not overtake him until the next day. So you see, Harmon, there wouldn't be much sense in going further into the matter. Now would there?'

'As if I haven't enough on my back. You were saying you'd like to leave with me for Laverton tonight.'

'Better have someone with you and the prisoner. He might slip the handcuffs!'

Harmon grinned. 'Yes, he might. Like young Tony, eh?

That's a yarn I have still to listen to. Shall we make it seven o'clock to pull out?'

'I've been working hard, too, Nat,' claimed Esther Harmon happily when her brother and the 'yardman' were eating her well-cooked dinner. 'I tackled Melody Sam about giving Tony a job, and he said he'd take him on as barman. I told him that wouldn't do. I said I couldn't have Tony working in any hotel. He shouted and I shouted.' Esther's dark eyes were actually illumined by her happiness. 'In the end he agreed to do what I suggested. He'll have Mrs Joyce in to look after him and his hotel, and he will hand over the butchering business to Tony the day he marries Joy Elder.'

'That's fine, Esther, and you will permit me to call you Esther after all this? What did you arrange for George?'

'Oh, he's to stay here at Daybreak, aren't you, George?'

'Don't know about that,' grumbled George.

'Oh, yes, you do. You told me lots of times you'd never leave Daybreak because there's no one here to train the kids properly.'

'You appear to have managed everyone very well, Esther,' Bony told her appreciatively. 'I cannot tell you how glad I am that you have found the son you have always wanted. Remember me to Tony and his bride-to-be.'

He found Sister Jenks sitting outside her house. The east wind was coming over the summit of Bulow's Range, and, after many quiet days, the music it played in the pepper trees was pleasing to the ear. Sister Jenks congratulated him, and expressed regret for having spoken so bluntly at their first meeting. Months later, when on holiday in Perth, she remembered what he then said to her.

'The circumstances were unusual, Sister. Whatever it was you said I don't remember. I had too much on my mind. *Au revoir!* And thanks for being my magnifying glass.'

To part from Melody Sam was the most difficult of all. Sam had implored Nat the yardman to stay on with him, and now when Bony had packed his swag and handed in the horse gear to Constable Harmon, he found Melody Sam down in the cellar under the bar, and the trap bolted.

Sam was playing his violin, and for a moment or two Bony stood quietly listening. The aborigines have a saying: 'It's hard for the old men to dig for water, but thirst gives them strength.' The music stopped and up through the boards came the remembered first line:

'Oh, come to me arms, me darlin'.'

'You come up here, Sam,' called Bony, and after a period of reflection, Sam shouted:

'Go away, Nat. Go back to your policemen. I wanted to give you a permanent job. I went as far as to say I'd give you the flaming pub. And you turned me down. Go away.'

'Not until you come up and say goodbye, Sam.'

'If you don't clear out, I'll blow you up, pub and all.'

'You can't, Sam.'

'Can't I? I got a case of gelly down here, and a detonator and fuse all set for a match.'

'I tricked you this time, Sam,' Bony declared. 'I took all the gelly out and put rubbish in. Look into the case and see.'

Sounds of activity reached Bony. Then the steps to the trap creaked. The bolt was shot back, and the trap was flung upward. There arose Melody Sam, to stand straight and steady and seemingly everlasting, like those broad-leafed mulgas.

Slowly he advanced, both gnarled hands outstretched. His white hair was ruffled, his white moustache needed to be clipped. It wasn't whisky which made his eyes abnormally bright.

'Goodbye, Nat. I'm a bit tired. I must be getting old. Can't take it like I used to. No kick in it any more. My last bender was that time you come to Daybreak and acted lovers with Kat. And now Kat's gone and you're going. So long, Nat. The best of luck.' His voice sank to a whisper. 'Get out of my pub, Nat. Go on; get out!'

NIGHT SKY
Clare Francis

A compelling adventure story of love and war with a finale that will become classic in epic storytelling.

When Clare Francis, one of the world's foremost solo yachtswomen, wrote her first novel, she took the world by storm with a tremendously powerful tale set in the turmoil of war-torn Europe.

A German scientist is forced by the Nazis to work on submarine radar that will save Admiral Doenitz's savage U-boat campaign. An Englishwoman, stranded in Brittany, has pledged to help him escape the tyranny of the régime that hates him because he is a Jew. All that stands between them and freedom is the English Channel. All they have to save them is a small, leaking, compass-less boat, beneath the night sky . . .

'A thriller of true love, sailboat rescue and wartime resistance . . . can't escape being a slam-bang bestseller'
Company

'Magic that is hard to describe. Perhaps it is simply that Clare Francis really knows what she is writing about when she writes about the sea'
Punch

Fiction

Options	Freda Bright
The Thirty-nine Steps	John Buchan
Secret of Blackoaks	Ashley Carter
Hercule Poirot's Christmas	Agatha Christie
Dupe	Liza Cody
Lovers and Gamblers	Jackie Collins
Sphinx	Robin Cook
Ragtime	E. L. Doctorow
My Cousin Rachel	Daphne du Maurier
Mr American	George Macdonald Fraser
The Moneychangers	Arthur Hailey
Secrets	Unity Hall
Black Sheep	Georgette Heyer
The Eagle Has Landed	Jack Higgins
Sins of the Fathers	Susan Howatch
The Master Sniper	Stephen Hunter
Smiley's People	John le Carré
To Kill a Mockingbird	Harper Lee
Ghosts	Ed McBain
Gone with the Wind	Margaret Mitchell
Blood Oath	David Morrell
Platinum Logic	Tony Parsons
Wilt	Tom Sharpe
Rage of Angels	Sidney Sheldon
The Unborn	David Shobin
A Town Like Alice	Nevile Shute
A Falcon Flies	Wilbur Smith
The Deep Well at Noon	Jessica Stirling
The Ironmaster	Jean Stubbs
The Music Makers	E. V. Thompson

Non-fiction

Extraterrestrial Civilizations	Isaac Asimov
Pregnancy	Gordon Bourne
Jogging From Memory	Rob Buckman
The 35mm Photographer's Handbook	Julian Calder and John Garrett
Travellers' Britain } **Travellers' Italy**	Arthur Eperon
The Complete Calorie Counter	Eileen Fowler

All these books are available at your local bookshop or newsagent.